Praise for *Libby of High Hopes, Project Blue Ribbon*

"Believable dialogue and vivid characterizations enhance the story, which Primavera illustrates with lively, sometimes amusing pen-and-ink drawings. A fine choice for fans of horses and riding, the second book in the Libby of High Hopes series is as enjoyable as the first."—*Booklist*

★ ★ ★ ★ ★

Praise for *Libby of High Hopes*

"Elise Primavera has created a young girl with family and friends so real you want to know them all. The journey through her summer is filled with soul and charm, simply wonderful."—Petra Mathers

"I wish I could take riding lessons at High Hopes Horse Farm with a friend just like Libby Thump. I was a lot like Libby Thump, always drawing horses and dreaming of riding them. If I'd known her when I was a kid, I'm sure we would have been best friends!"

—Marissa Moss, author of *Amelia's Notebook*

"A fresh story with some good life lessons and well developed characters (including the horses). We hope that Primavera will give us more about Libby very soon." —Kidsreads.com

"Expressive full-page illustrations appear throughout. The well written story teaches a gentle lesson that life can be unfair, but persistence and passion payoff." —*School Library Journal*

"A solid choice for horse lovers ready to move past early chapter books." —*Kirkus Reviews*

"The wide-spaced lines of type and vivid black-and-white drawings make this an accessible, attractive choice for younger chapter-book readers. Primavera offers a nuanced story that acknowledges some of the painful parts of childhood without letting them diminish Libby's resilient nature."

—*Booklist*

Also by Elise Primavera

The Secret Order of the Gumm Street Girls

Auntie Claus series

Ms. Rapscott's Girls

Libby of High Hopes

LIBBY of HIGH HOPES

★ PROJECT BLUE RIBBON ★

• STORY AND PICTURES BY •

ELISE PRIMAVERA

A Paula Wiseman Book
Simon & Schuster Books for Young Readers
New York London Toronto Sydney New Delhi

SIMON & SCHUSTER BOOKS FOR YOUNG READERS
An imprint of Simon & Schuster Children's Publishing Division
1230 Avenue of the Americas, New York, New York 10020

Also available in a Simon & Schuster Books for Young Readers hardcover edition
Book design by Krista Vossen
The text for this book was set in Stempel Garamond.
The illustrations for this book were rendered in pen and ink.
Manufactured in the United States of America
0816 OFF
First Simon & Schuster Books for Young Readers paperback edition September 2016
2 4 6 8 10 9 7 5 3 1
The Library of Congress has cataloged the hardcover edition as follows:
Primavera, Elise.
Libby of High Hopes : Project Blue Ribbon / Elise Primavera.
pages cm
"A Paula Wiseman book."
Summary: "There is only one way for Libby to live up to her potential and achieve
her dream of being the best rider in the world. Find a way to win a Blue Ribbon with
Saddleshoes, the most difficult pony at High Hopes Farm"—Provided by publisher.
ISBN 978-1-4169-5543-6 (hc)
[1. Horses—Fiction. 2. Horsemanship—Fiction. 3. Horse shows—Fiction.]
I. Title. II. Title: Project Blue Ribbon.
PZ7.P9354Lj 2015
[Fic]—dc23
2014048129
ISBN 978-1-4169-5545-0 (pbk)
ISBN 978-1-4424-5220-6 (eBook)

For my aunt, Kate Maple,

whose deep love for animals,

especially horses and dogs,

knows no bounds

LIBBY THE RIDER

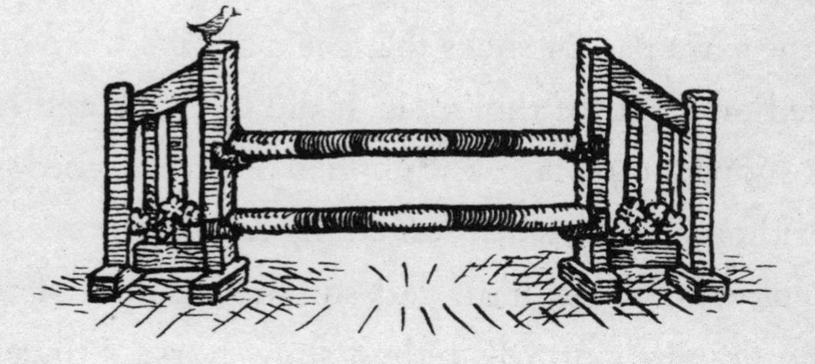

Libby Thump wished for a blue ribbon. A satin royal blue ribbon with a rosette and the words “First Place” written in gold lettering. There was going to be a horse show in three weeks and that’s exactly where she hoped to win one. Libby was excited because Sal, who owned High Hopes Horse Farm, was supposed to tell her today if he thought she was ready to ride in the show.

She sat on the floor of her bedroom trying to pull

on her left boot. "Come on," she said impatiently, but it wouldn't budge. She'd grown an inch since last summer and the riding boots that had been handed down from her sister were beginning to get tight. She yanked off the extra pair of socks that she'd always worn and pulled on a pair of thin ones. It did the trick and her foot slipped into place. She jumped up and reached for her riding helmet, when something caught her eye.

Libby tilted her head and squinted at one of the many drawings of Sal's retired show horse, Princess, she'd taped to the wall. She suddenly noticed for the first time there was something wrong with the way she'd drawn the white mare and grabbed an eraser and pencil off her table to fix it.

"*Libbyyyyyyyy!*" her mother called to her. "Please walk the dog!"

"In a minute!" Libby called back. Margaret gazed up at her and wagged her tail expectantly. Libby got the leash—the drawing would have to wait—but as she turned to leave she caught a reflection of herself in the mirror. There were the same long dark braids, dark eyes, and oval face, but in her boots and jeans and quilted vest she looked like a real rider! Libby wondered what her fourth-grade teacher from last year would think of her now. Libby remembered what Mrs. Williams had written on Libby's report card the last day of school.

Libby needs to apply herself. Sometimes she does not pay attention or follow directions as well as she should. Libby needs to live up to her potential!

Back then Libby wasn't even sure what potential was. By now she had memorized the meaning of the word: "something that can develop or become actual." Libby knew just what that "something" was, too; she was a rider! It was what she was meant to be. She just hoped that she had the potential to someday become a really good rider. She thought she could feel it in there, just itching to get out!

Sure enough, a lot had changed since Mrs. Williams's class. Throughout the fall and all winter Libby had been riding Princess, and she was even learning to jump.

Libby moved her face closer to the mirror. She sucked in her cheeks and tried to imagine what she would look like when she was grown up. Would she be a really good rider by then? Did she have what it would take?

"*Libbyyyyy!*" her mother called again.

Libby glanced at the clock on her night table. "Oh my gosh!" she cried, and raced out of the room with Margaret scrambling behind her. "Laurel! Laurel!" Libby pressed the leash into her sister's hands. "I've got a lesson—I don't want to be late—just this once, please? Thanks!"

Libby tore out of the house. Her sister stamped her foot and yelled, "*Libbyyyyyy!*"

Libby pretended she didn't hear and ran as fast as she could through the park to the path in the woods. She never stopped till she stood in the grassy field on top of the same hill as in the pictures that she'd covered her bedroom walls with. "Princess! Come on, girl!"

Below the horse nickered and soon there was a

thunder of hooves. The white mare's mane whipped in the wind as she galloped up to meet the girl. She skidded to a stop and nudged Libby's pocket for a carrot.

Libby jogged down the hill and Princess followed behind like an enormous dog. There was the smell of damp earth and new grass. All winter Libby had been looking forward to spring and now it was finally here. She breathed in deeply and sighed. The sky was blue and the air was just beginning to have the first hint of warmth.

At the gate she grabbed the halter and slipped it over the mare's nose. "This has to be our best lesson yet, Princess!" Libby knew that she would have to ride extra-specially well this day in order for Sal to think that she was good enough to compete in the horse show.

As soon as they entered the barn Brittany poked her head out of a stall where she was tacking up Summer, the horse she always rode. Libby's and Brittany's moms were best friends and that had automatically made Libby and Brittany best friends since they were babies. They'd had a "misunderstanding" last year, but now Libby was glad they were best friends again.

"Lesson today?" Brittany asked.

"Yep!" Libby grinned as she passed.

At the end of the aisle was one of Sal's boarders, Mr. McClave and his horse, General George. "Hi, Mr. McClave!" Libby shouted.

The old man paused from brushing off his horse. "All ready for your lesson?"

"All ready!" Libby answered, and secured Princess to the cross ties. She hurried to the tack room.

A blond curly-haired woman in jeans and hacking boots bustled down the aisle with several flakes of hay that she threw into stalls. Emily was Sal's wife and helped him run the stable.

"Hi, Emily!" Libby called to her.

"Libby!" Emily called back. "Sal will be right out!"

"Great!" Libby grabbed her saddle and bridle and felt the butterflies in her stomach that were always there right before she was to have a jumping lesson. She still couldn't pass by the photos in the tack room of Sal riding the big white horse over the gigantic fences without getting goose bumps. Now here she was, Libby Thump, jumping Princess herself.

She was so anxious to get out to the ring that it was all she could do to take the time to pick out each of the mare's hooves and then brush her off and tack her up. Libby's fingers nervously fumbled with the snaps on her riding helmet. All ready, she led Princess down the aisle.

She wanted everything to go well this afternoon.

Brittany poked her head out of Summer's stall again, "Watch out for Saddleshoes!"

"Oh no!" Libby groaned.

"Oh yes!" Brittany said.

Outside Libby could see that Brittany was right. There was Saddleshoes. With his dazzling white legs, brown spots on his neck and rump, and a handsome blaze down the front of his face Saddleshoes was the best-looking pony around. But . . . as far as Libby was concerned he was also the worst pony there ever was.

Libby entered the ring careful to steer Princess far away from him, for he could deliver a mean kick. Suddenly there was a gust of wind and Saddleshoes spooked to the side. Somewhere the sound of a tractor started up and he shied and tried to buck.

His rider, Kate, was eighteen and small for her age, which was why she was still able to ride a large pony. She was also a talented and fearless rider and the only one who could control Saddleshoes.

Throughout all of the pony's shenanigans Princess remained quiet and steady. She paid absolutely no attention to Saddleshoes when he flattened his ears at her.

Kate gathered her reins and headed him toward a fence. Libby walked Princess around to the far corner of the ring to get out of the way. The spotted pony leaped off at a ferocious speed. Libby could barely look. Kate tried to hold him. He raised his head and fought her with every stride but somehow he met the

fence perfectly. He could jump beautifully, but Libby knew that before Kate bought the pony from Sal, when other kids rode Saddleshoes, it was a completely different story. He would rush his fences only to slam on the brakes at the last minute. A "dirty stop," Sal called it, because the pony did it so quickly and for no reason.

"Good boy!" Kate praised him, and leaned over to pat his neck.

Libby frowned. So far this afternoon was not going at all the way she'd wanted it to. She could just see stupid Saddleshoes charging right in front of Princess as they tried to jump a fence, or worse, kick her if she got too close—you just never knew with that pony. He was unpredictable. Libby looked around for Sal and hoped that he would make them leave, when she noticed a lone girl leaning on the fence. She was standing next to a short, squat, dark-haired woman—probably the girl's mother. There were always kids—mostly girls—hanging around the barn, but Libby had never seen this girl before. She had a solemn, oblong face, long poker-straight light brown Alice in Wonderland hair with bangs across her high forehead. The girl's stern expression reminded Libby of the kind she'd seen on adults right before they were about to tell her not to do something.

As Libby went by, the girl said, "I like your horse," in a surprisingly shy tone of voice.

"Thanks, but she's not mine," Libby replied.

Kate and Saddleshoes jumped over another fence and Libby held her breath. It made her so nervous to watch him. He went for Kate because she was a fantastic rider, but he stopped or tried to run away with every other kid Libby had ever seen try to ride him. She didn't know why he was so bad. All Libby knew was that she was glad *she* didn't have to ride him. Libby wished again that Kate and Saddleshoes would leave the ring. She didn't want them to ruin her jumping lesson today of all days.

What Libby didn't know was that one of her worst fears was about to come true.

2

LIBBY'S WORST FEAR COMES TRUE

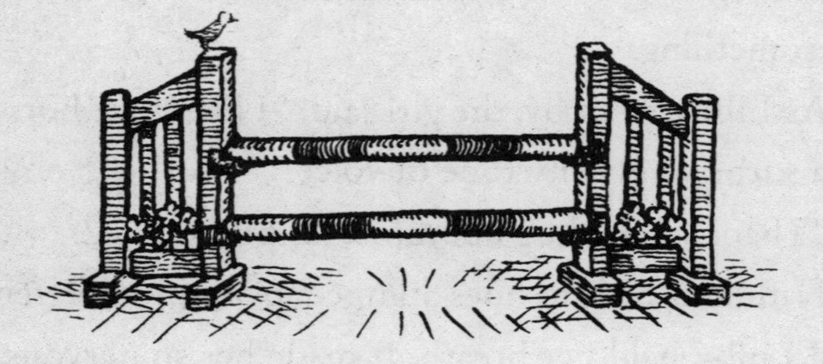

"Shorten your reins, Libby!" Sal entered the ring. With his craggy, weathered face and jet-black hair he always reminded Libby of a pirate. Libby saw him walk to the center with the familiar limp he'd been left with from the riding accident he'd had jumping Princess years ago. Libby shortened her reins and sat up a little taller. She glanced around to see where Saddleshoes and Kate were.

"Libby! Pay attention!" Sal called out to her. Libby

did her best now to concentrate. Sal asked her to circle, and he was real stickler about the size and shape of each one. "Look in the direction that you're going, Libby!" Libby looked over her shoulder to the center of the circle. "Good!" He sounded happier. She had to do transitions: go from a trot to a walk, then halt, then back to a trot.

"Canter," Sal said after she'd been trotting for ten minutes. Princess had a canter that was easy to sit to and Libby hardly had to do anything to circle her around the ring.

"Trot!" Sal ordered. "Get in your jumping position."

Libby had already practiced this many times on Princess since she first started to learn to jump in the fall. In the beginning it had been hard to stand in her stirrups while Princess was trotting. Libby had grabbed the mane to balance herself and to keep her seat from falling back into the saddle, but over the months she had gotten better at it. Now it was easy.

"Keep your weight in your stirrups, Libby!" Sal reminded her and began to place some poles on the ground that he called "cavaletti." "Turn left and trot over the poles."

Libby's jumping lessons always started with cavalettis. Princess was a pro and trotted right through them, lifting her legs a little higher in an even tempo.

Sal next put a small crossbar after the poles. Princess hopped over it easily. Libby knew what would come next—another fence after the crossbar to create what was called an in-and-out.

"Alternate turning left and right after the jump," Sal

ordered. Libby was still only allowed to trot at this point in the lesson but she knew she would start to canter fences soon, and that was her favorite part. She posted over the poles on the ground, and Princess took a stride, Libby leaned forward, and they jumped the "in," then the mare took another stride and jumped the "out."

"Good job!" Sal said. Libby grinned. She and Princess were doing really well today. She couldn't wait to canter the fences!

"Make a circle at the canter and come over the brush

box," Sal directed. "Get her in straight. . . . Good!"

Princess always came into her fences at the same speed, which made it easier for Libby to tell exactly where the mare was going to take off. Libby knew she needed to stay balanced in the saddle and concentrate on her position: keep her head up, her heels down, and her back straight.

"Keep her at the canter, now," Sal said. He gave her several fences to jump, making sure that she had turns and changes of direction. This was the same sort of course that Libby would have in a horse show. As she jumped each fence Sal helped her. "Make a wider turn, Libby," he warned. "Keep your hands down. . . . Look up!" Libby knew the lesson was almost over.

"Okay, now come over the gate!" Sal said.

Libby came around the corner, one . . . two . . . three . . . jump! Princess took off over the fence, they were up in the air, and it was like flying!

"There's my good little jockey!" Sal praised Libby, and she grinned from ear to ear. Sal didn't hand out compliments too often, but when he did Libby loved it because she knew he really meant it and that she had ridden well. He called her into the center of the ring.

It had gone exactly the way Libby had hoped it would. Sal had to think she was ready to ride Princess in the show in a few weeks. She *would* win a blue ribbon—maybe even a championship!

Kate walked Saddleshoes over to join Libby and Sal. Libby marveled that she had forgotten that they were even in the ring!

But there was something wrong. The older girl looked down; her shoulders sagged as she stroked the pony's neck. Had Libby been so caught up in her jumping lesson that she'd missed something? What had the awful pony done now? Had he stopped with her at a fence? Had he shied? Or tried to run away with her? Had Kate finally had enough? Libby knew *she* would have had enough a long time ago. Saddleshoes gave Libby a dirty look as if he knew she was thinking bad thoughts about him.

"Libby, hop off Princess for a minute. I have a surprise for you," Sal said.

"A surprise?" Libby hesitated and then dismounted.

Sal whispered mysteriously, "You'll see."

Kate got off the pony. "So I guess this is good-bye, Sal." Her voice sounded a little sad.

"Are you leaving?" Libby said incredulously.

"I'm going down south to spend some time at my aunt's farm," Kate said.

Sal smiled. "It's a great opportunity."

"I'll have the chance to ride lots of different horses," Kate added. Everyone knew that instead of going right to college Kate had taken a year off to see if she wanted to pursue a career in riding horses.

Libby was sorry to see Kate go but she wasn't a bit sorry to see her pony go. "You're taking Saddleshoes, right?" It was hard for her to not sound excited at the prospect of Saddleshoes leaving.

"Not right now," Kate said. "If everything works out I'll come back at some point and take him down there to stay with me." Kate exchanged a knowing look with Sal. "In the meantime he'll be in good hands." Then Kate did something that was probably the worst thing that could ever happen: She handed the reins to Libby.

Libby froze.

Sal laughed. "Kate has decided—and I agree—that *you* should ride Saddleshoes." Kate stood with a big smile and an outstretched hand, offering Libby the reins while Libby hung on to Princess's reins with all her might. "But—but, what about Princess?"

Sal took Princess from Libby and she could have sworn that Princess gave her a worried look. She couldn't help feeling as though the ground beneath her very feet had just dropped out from under her and she was free-falling to some terrible place.

"Princess can't take a lot of work, Libby, you know that." Sal smoothed the mare's forelock as he spoke. "She's getting old, and all this jumping is going to eventually make her lame."

Dark clouds were forming in the west and the wind suddenly switched direction. When Libby looked, the strange girl who'd been leaning on the rail at the end of

the ring and her mother were gone. The beautiful spring day had vanished. Libby shivered.

"You need a horse you can jump more often," Sal said firmly. "And the best part is that while Kate's away it'll be like having your own pony—just what you've always wanted."

Libby reached out a hand to pet Saddleshoes. He laid back his ears at her and a tingle of dread slithered up her spine.

"You're going to learn a lot from this pony," Sal said confidently.

Libby turned to Kate. "But no one can ride Saddleshoes except you."

"And *you*," Kate said good-naturedly. She linked her arm in Libby's.

Libby bit her lip—she had to ask, "How do you do it, Kate?"

"He taught me how." Kate stroked the pony's neck.

"Saddleshoes?" Libby didn't believe it.

Sal nodded. "Some of the most difficult horses—and ponies—make the best teachers."

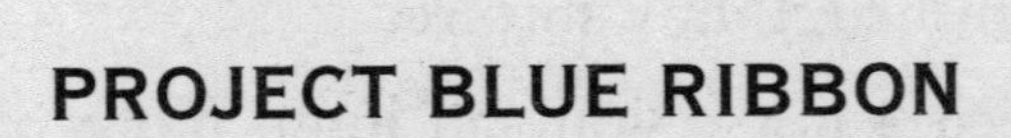

3

PROJECT BLUE RIBBON

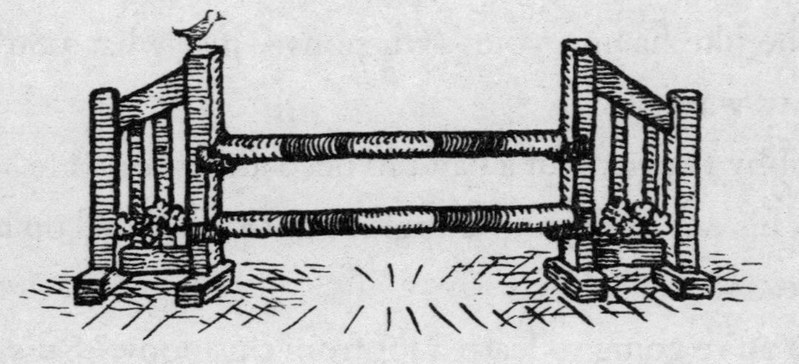

The sun was going down and Libby zipped her vest up to her chin. How could so much change in just the blink of an eye? She kicked a stone out of the way as she led Princess back to her paddock. "Just when everything was going so well," Libby muttered.

She slipped the halter off Princess and looked into the mare's eyes, which seemed to say, *I'm old, Libby, you knew this day would come*. Libby put her arms around Princess's neck, closed her eyes, and hugged her. She *had* known the day would come. In fact when she first came to High Hopes Horse Farm, Princess was just turned out in the field all the time. Libby had cleaned her up and Sal had agreed to let her ride the horse, but he had told her right from the start that Princess couldn't take a lot of work. Libby knew she'd feel absolutely awful if Princess had gone lame while she was riding her—best to stop before that happened.

"Sal is right, girl. We can't do anything that will hurt you." Libby leaned over and ran a hand down one of the horse's front legs. She could feel the lumps and bumps Princess had accumulated from all the hard work of showing and jumping, which only confirmed that Sal was right.

She scratched behind the mare's ears. "Besides, you've already won hundreds of blue ribbons. I'll bet you don't feel like you need any more, do you?" Libby fed Princess the last carrot from her pocket and turned to go.

The horse followed Libby up the hill to the post and

rail fence. She reached out her nose and Libby kissed it. "It's okay, girl, I'm fine. Don't worry about me." She didn't want Princess to know how disappointed she was, but as soon as Libby got home she marched into her room, dug through her backpack, and found the beaten-up old notebook that she brought with her everywhere. On the cover in blue glitter she had written:

PROJECT BLUE RIBBON

In it she had charted her progress toward the one goal that she'd had since the first day she rode the big white jumper. Written on the first page was:

Win a blue ribbon
on Princess!!!

Libby sat cross-legged on her bed and leafed through all the pages of days leading up to this one. There was the first time, when she'd written all about how she'd cantered Princess; the first time she'd trotted over a pole on the ground; and the first time she'd trotted over a real jump.

Libby's eyes welled up with tears because she couldn't believe that her days of riding Princess were really over and that she would now be faced with riding the worst pony on earth.

It wasn't fair.

That night it was a normal Sunday. The TV was on and everyone was gathered in the family room eating pizza. Libby picked at her food, sighed, and fed Margaret bits of pizza until her father finally said, "That's enough, Libby. You're cleaning it up if that dog gets sick."

Libby's mother looked at her with concern. "Don't you feel well, honey?"

"I'm fine," Libby said in a voice that sounded anything but.

Mrs. Thump got up from her chair and placed a

hand on her daughter's forehead. "You don't seem to have a fever."

Laurel smirked. "Big test tomorrow? Square dancing? What?"

Libby took a deep breath, exhaled loudly, and broke the news to her family. "Sal said I'm not going to be able to ride Princess, that she can't take a lot of riding and jumping anymore."

Libby's parents weren't surprised. "Honey, you knew that Princess was getting on in years," her father said sympathetically.

Libby closed her eyes and nodded. She *had* known, but that didn't make it any easier. She began to explain. "You know Kate and Saddleshoes?"

Laurel answered, "She's that really good rider who bought Sal's crazy brown-and-white pony." Laurel had taken riding lessons all last summer while Libby watched, but she had stopped when school started up. She still went over to the barn occasionally to talk to Emily, though she rarely rode anymore. She was more interested in clothes and boys these days. "That pony is nuts!"

Libby stared at Laurel and tried to convey with her eyes for her sister to, *Zip it!* Then she talked fast in the hopes that her parents hadn't picked up on Laurel's comment. "So, Kate is going to her aunt's farm to ride for a few months, and while she's gone I'm—um, in charge of Saddleshoes."

Laurel's eyes popped open wide and she mouthed the words, *To ride?!*

Her parents had seen. Libby looked up at the ceiling in exasperation at her sister. If her parents knew of Saddleshoes's awful reputation they might not let her ride him—then she'd have no horse to ride at all.

"Saddleshoes is nuts?" Libby's mother sounded worried.

Libby quickly came to Saddleshoes's defense. "He's not *nuts*—he's just a little . . . um, frisky." Libby turned to her sister. "Right, Laurel?"

"Right, right . . . not nuts—frisky," Laurel said, her eyes down.

Libby nodded, relieved that her sister had finally caught on. She waved her hand. "I can handle him—and besides, while Kate is gone it will be just like having my own pony."

"Well that's . . . wonderful," Mrs. Thump said a little hesitantly. "As long as you're sure he's safe to ride."

"I can totally handle him," Libby said confidently. "And you know the old saying. . . . 'Never look a gift pony in the mouth.'" Everyone laughed and seemed to relax.

But later Laurel came to Libby's room. She leaned against the dresser and spoke in a low voice. "I still say that pony is *nuts*." Laurel pointed her index finger at the side of head and twirled it. "He's, like, got wheels in his head and they're all going the wrong way—I mean, he bucks off every kid that gets on him. No one can ride him except Kate. Are you sure you know what you're doing, Libby?"

"Sure, I'm sure," Libby said breezily, though she had never been less sure of anything in her life.

4

PROBLEMS

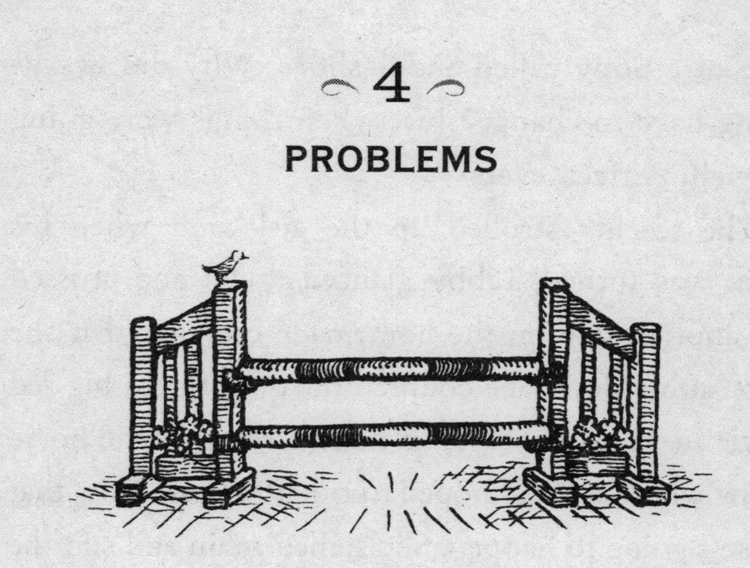

The next day Libby sat in class and tried to look as though she was paying attention. Her teacher, Mr. Kaufman, read a math word problem, "If Donovan rides his bike two and a half miles to the park, then three and three quarters miles to the candy store, and then to his friend Logan's house, which is half the distance of both destinations combined, and then . . ."

Libby sighed. She had a much bigger problem than Donovan's bike ride. She had a problem the size of a pony called Saddleshoes. Why did everything have to change? Just when things were going so well. Perfect, even.

The teacher strolled up the aisle and when his back was turned, Libby glanced down and crossed off another day on the homemade calendar that she kept in her desk. She counted the days to the big red circle in May—the date in three weeks for the horse show where she had hoped to ride Princess. Now that wasn't going to happen. She sighed again and slid the calendar back into her desk.

The cover of Libby's notebook was filled with drawings of Saddleshoes, with his mean little ears that pointed in and looked just like the horns of a devil. She drew a smile on his face but it only made him look more diabolical. Sal believed she could ride Saddleshoes, so she had to believe she could. But could she? She squeezed her eyes shut and remembered that her mother had always said the most important thing was to try . . . to try . . . to try . . . to try . . .

"Libby?"

Libby blinked.

Mr. Kaufman was speaking to her. Everybody was staring at her. "How many miles did Donovan ride his bike?"

Libby looked over at Brittany helplessly.

Brittany had her hands in her lap and furtively held up all her fingers, where Mr. Kaufman couldn't see.

"Um . . . ten?" Libby answered in a small voice.

Mr. Kaufman narrowed his eyes, looking at her. "Correct, Miss Thump, but— " Just then the bell rang. It was eleven thirty. Libby grabbed her lunch and hurried from the room before her teacher could nab her and deliver the lecture about how she needed to pay more attention. Again.

Nope. Nothing had changed from fourth grade to fifth. Last year Mrs. Williams didn't think Libby paid enough attention either. Of course they were both right—Libby knew she *didn't* pay enough attention. As she made her way to the cafeteria she wondered, *was paying attention like riding? Was it something that you could practice? If she practiced would she get better at it?*

She sat at her usual table eating her sandwich silently, churning this over and over in her mind. Libby didn't notice Brittany and Libby's other best friend, Mim, had stopped talking.

"Hi, I'm Amanda," a voice said. Libby looked up and there was an outstretched hand in her face.

"You were by the ring at High Hopes Horse Farm yesterday," Libby said through a mouthful of tuna fish.

"You did really well in your jumping lesson," Amanda said nicely. "That's a fantastic horse you're riding. You must be very pleased."

"*Pleased?*" Brittany said mockingly. Libby thought it was just the sort of nerdy expression that Brittany wouldn't like.

Amanda seemed not to hear the comment, which Libby thought was pretty amazing since everyone

always hung on Brittany's every word. The girl tilted her head and directed her question to Libby. "I wanted to ask you—how much are riding lessons?"

Libby noticed that Amanda had a way of standing with her back erect and her arms crossed protectively over her chest. Her feet were planted firmly on the ground with her legs locked at the knee, which made her look very bow-legged, like she'd been riding a horse for too long. For a kid she seemed very serious and possibly the kind that annoyingly always had her hand up first in class and got along better with grown-ups—still, there was something about this odd girl that made Libby want to give her a chance.

"Do you even know how to ride?" Brittany asked.

Amanda pulled in her chin toward her neck. There was the stern adult expression that Libby remembered from the other day. "Yes. I've been riding for a while."

Brittany raised her eyebrows and said, *"A while?"*

"Oh boy. Here we go," Mim said under her breath. She knew how Brittany could be if she thought another kid might be better than her at something.

Libby came to Amanda's rescue. "You need to bring your parents to High Hopes and have them talk to Sal. He can help you with lessons."

"Okay." Amanda nodded and walked away stiffly.

"What was *that* all about?" Brittany said.

"She was at the barn yesterday," Libby replied.

All three girls watched as Amanda made her way over to the fourth-grade section to eat her lunch.

Brittany and Mim craned their necks to see the strange girl who seemed totally unconcerned to sit down alone at a table. Nobody sat alone in the cafeteria unless they had no friends or were new.

"She must be new," Mim muttered. "Poor kid."

"I think she's weird." Brittany shrugged. "Whatever." Now that she knew Amanda was a fourth grader, she was no longer interested in her.

Amanda took out a book. She read as she ate her lunch all by herself and Libby couldn't help feeling sorry for the younger girl. She knew that Brittany could be mean sometimes, like last summer when she didn't pick Libby—because she was so slow—to be on her swim team in the relay race. Suddenly Libby found herself hoping that Amanda *would* start riding at the barn. It would be fun to show someone new all the different horses at High Hopes and tell her what was special about each one. Libby could introduce Amanda to Mr. McClave and General George and Princess and . . . Saddleshoes.

Libby could feel her stomach tighten. Saddleshoes, the problem pony, came galloping back into her mind. Yes, it would be fun to show Amanda all around High Hopes Horse Farm and introduce her to Saddleshoes—that is, if Libby ever survived riding him this afternoon.

5

LIBBY'S IDEA

Libby was out of her school clothes, into her barn clothes, and had walked Margaret before her mother or her sister could even start to nag her about it. Soon she was standing in front of the brown-and-white pony's stall, her mouth dry, her heart pounding, and her sister's words still ringing in her ears: *He's nuts. . . . No one can ride him except Kate*. As soon as she got closer Saddleshoes immediately turned his rump to her, and Libby backed away.

"Sal? Emily?" She wasn't about to start without help. They weren't in the ring teaching, or in the tack room. She went around to the large shed where they kept all the hay and shavings. Sal's truck was positioned as if he'd been unloading hay, and there he was in a discussion with Emily.

Something in Emily's posture and Sal's drawn face made Libby not want to interrupt them, so she decided to slip behind several bales of shavings and hide to watch and listen.

Emily placed one hand on Sal's shoulder and delivered the bad news. She told him they had lost another boarder to a fancier stable.

Sal yanked off his gloves. Libby could see his hands were rough and veined from years of carrying water buckets, mucking stalls, and grooming horses. He shook his head with frustration. "You would think that after all the years that I've been working with horses I wouldn't have this trouble keeping boarders."

Emily pressed her lips together. "You know we

didn't get into the horse business to make money, Sal," she said gently.

"It's not just money, Emily," Sal said. "It's my reputation."

Emily furrowed her brow.

Libby knew that Sal had been one of the top riders in the country until he'd had the crash over a fence at a show with Princess some years back. For a while it looked like High Hopes Horse Farm would never recover. Then last year Emily started to show again and the students and boarders came back. But there was no indoor ring at the old farm and people had left over the winter. So far they hadn't come back.

"Everyone thinks I'm washed up, I guess." Sal looked down.

"Since when do you care what everyone thinks?" Emily said jokingly, but Sal didn't laugh. "You can't let it get to you, Sal."

"I know," Sal muttered. Then he and Emily went back to unloading hay.

Libby stole away from her hiding place and walked to the barn with a heavy heart. Saddleshoes did not have his head over the stall door to greet her with a nicker the way Princess always did. Libby rolled the door to the side and the cantankerous pony glared at her from the shadows. She stood face-to-face with him, thinking.

Sal can't compete at shows over the big fences any-more but he's still an incredible instructor and Emily's a fantastic rider. Why can't people see that? Libby frowned. *If only I was still riding Princess I would go to that show and win a slew of blue ribbons. Maybe then people would see what a great teacher Sal really is. Maybe then people would come back and want to take lessons at High Hopes Farm and board their horses!*

But she wasn't riding Princess. *All I have to ride now is stupid Saddleshoes*, Libby thought glumly. She could never win a blue ribbon riding him.

Or could she? The pony watched her warily from his corner of the stall, and Libby watched him while an image formed in her mind. She was riding the pony at the show, the loudspeaker announcing, "In first place is Libby Thump, riding Saddleshoes!"

Oh, it's just a dream, Libby thought. *Probably impossible.* She knew it was . . . but she closed her eyes and crossed her fingers anyway. "I wish I could win a blue ribbon riding Saddleshoes," she whispered to herself.

There. It was done. She had wished it. It could never be taken back.

Libby entered the stall with renewed determination. Every time she got near Saddleshoes with the halter he turned his hindquarters to her. She offered him a carrot, which he took, but just as quickly he spun around and they were back where they started from. She ran out of carrots and got some grain. When he shoved his nose in the bucket she threw the lead shank around his neck. "Gotcha!" she said, and buckled up his halter.

That wasn't so bad, Libby thought, and she clipped him to the cross-ties but Saddleshoes wouldn't stand still. He moved forward and backward and side to side. He tried to bite her when she curried him, and when she went to brush off his face he flew backward, broke his halter, and ran to his stall. Emily came to help and they were both able to get his saddle on. "Somebody has to hold his head while you do up the girth because he'll try to bite you," Emily said breathlessly. She cinched up the girth slightly and sure enough Saddleshoes reached around and tried to nip.

Libby hadn't even ridden the pony yet and she could already feel herself sweating under her vest, but she had made up her mind. She didn't know quite how, but she was determined to learn how to ride Saddleshoes, and then she was going to help Sal get his boarders back!

She ignored the pony's jigging and snorting on the way out to the mounting block. Even with Emily holding the reins it took three tries before she managed to get him to stand long enough so that she could get on. Luckily Sal came into the ring right behind her.

He seemed lost in thought and the lines in his forehead seemed deeper than ever before.

"Stay by me at the top of the ring, Libby," Sal said, and then looked over his shoulder. Libby followed his gaze to see Emily leading Sal's school pony, Cough Drop, into the ring.

Riding him was Amanda. Coming behind them was the short, squat, dark-haired woman from the day before, who Libby could hear talking a mile a minute.

"You don't need to lead her, for Pete's sake! She's been riding since she was three!" The woman laughed and then barked, "Amanda! Sit up straight! And fix your reins—what's the matter with you?" Emily didn't listen and led the pony into the ring. The woman took a place at the rail. She held the girl's jacket, a crop, and her handbag, which kept falling off her shoulder. "Amanda is a *very* experienced rider, you'll see."

"Mom," Amanda protested, embarrassed.

Sal nodded and Emily let the pony go.

"Honestly, Amanda! Sit. Up. Straight!" Amanda's mother snapped. "*Show* them how well you ride."

Libby cringed. If her mother ever said stuff like that she'd be mortified. As Libby was having this thought, suddenly for no apparent reason, Saddleshoes dropped a shoulder and shied. Libby grappled for the reins to pull him up, but he bolted to the other side of the ring.

"Libby!" She could barely hear Sal's voice over the rush of wind and the pounding of her own heartbeat in her ears. "Stay up at this end of the ring."

Libby could feel her face get red.

"You *have* to pay attention," Sal warned. "You're not riding Princess!"

Yeah, no kidding, Libby thought grimly. Princess had always taken such good care of her, it was like she was Libby's guardian angel, but Saddleshoes was like sitting on a stick of dynamite—the two were complete opposites! Libby felt as if she had never ridden before in her entire life.

She made her way over to Sal and Amanda, who was now walking on her own, and Libby thought the younger girl rode pretty well. Her heels were down; her hands were in the correct position. Sal called out, "Both of you, trot around me."

Libby was used to Princess, who picked up the trot with a slight squeeze of the leg. A slight squeeze of the leg on Saddleshoes could get you bucked into outer space. Libby panicked. What would he do if she asked him to trot?

"Keep your leg on him, Libby," Sal said.

Impossible, Libby thought. The pony felt like he was about to explode any minute.

"Better forget the trot for now," Sal said. He could see the trouble Libby was having. "Just walk."

Libby concentrated with every fiber of her being on trying to get the pony to "just walk" while Sal worked with Amanda. He was instructing her to do the same familiar circles and transitions that Libby had always done on Princess. As Saddleshoes continued to jig,

Libby couldn't help but notice that Amanda was doing remarkably well.

"Let her jump!" Amanda's mother cupped a hand at the side of her mouth and called out to Sal after they'd been going around for ten minutes.

Jump? Cough Drop? No one *ever* jumped Cough Drop. Just getting the pony to trot was a feat of Herculean proportions. Cough Drop was only used for the most beginner riders and so he knew all of the school pony tricks of the trade. He yanked the reins out of little kids' hands and galloped off to eat grass, or ran for the gate in an effort to get away and go back to the barn. His favorite thing was to trot at a snail's pace as if he were so tired, he could barely lift a hoof off the ground. No, Cough Drop did not jump.

"Trot him over the cavaletti," Sal said. Amanda pointed the pony at the same rails and crossbar that only yesterday Libby had gone over with Princess. To Libby's utter surprise Cough Drop trotted right though them and hopped over the crossbar.

"Good!" Even Sal seemed surprised.

The woman at the rail yelled out, "Give her a course to do!"

Libby knew that if there was one thing that Cough Drop hated more than jumping one fence, it was jumping two in a row. So when Sal told Amanda to take Cough Drop over eight fences in a twisty course, Libby doubted the pony would ever make it past the second jump.

Amanda gathered her reins and gave him a sharp kick. The pony's eyes snapped open wide as if a bucket of cold water had just been dumped on his head. Amanda kicked furiously to get Cough Drop to canter to the first fence. He heaved himself over it. When he tried to walk after this enormous effort, Amanda pushed him even harder. And it worked. Cough Drop never knew what hit him. Her loose pigtails streaming out behind her, she kicked and prodded the pony over those eight fences as if her life depended on it. Amanda was a good rider. Libby was impressed.

“Very, *very* good!” Sal laughed with delight. He patted the pony’s neck, and Cough Drop stood with his sides heaving, trying to catch his breath.

Libby was amazed. She’d never seen anyone ride Cough Drop like that, and suddenly she had another great idea. What if Amanda rode Cough Drop in the horse show and won a blue ribbon too? And what about Brittany? She won at everything—she could easily win on Summer. With three star pupils winning blue ribbons, people would *have* to notice High Hopes Horse Farm!

Saddleshoes had been just as awful as she thought he’d be, but as Libby left the ring that day she smiled. “Project Blue Ribbon” was officially being changed to “Project Blue Ribbons.” This was possibly the best idea she’d ever had!

YOU SNOOZE YOU LOSE!

No way!" Brittany stood in her gym uniform, gawking at Libby.

"Way," Libby answered. She was anxious to tell Brittany about Project Blue Ribbons but Brittany wouldn't give her the chance.

"That nerdy Amanda kid?" Brittany said with disbelief.

"Jumped Cough Drop," Libby answered.

The girls were in gym class waiting for the start of a

relay race. The relay race was not Libby's sport—neither was swimming, gymnastics, or ballet. In fact all Libby was good at so far was riding horses and drawing.

TWEET! TWEET! The gym teacher, Mrs. Whirly, blew her whistle and then shouted, "Go!" The girl in front of Libby took off with the baton that they were supposed to pass to each other. Kids hollered and sneakers squeaked on the floor as they sprinted and turned across the cavernous gym.

"Big deal," Brittany said, trying to sound unimpressed. "Anybody can ride Cough Drop."

"Over eight fences? In a row?" Libby shook her head. "Trust me, she's good."

"Well that's really great," Mim said cheerfully, and got into position to receive the baton from the next kid. "I mean, that Amanda's a good rider, right? Right?"

Libby knew that Mim was nicer than she was. In fact of all Libby's friends, Mim was probably the nicest. She was definitely nicer than Brittany, who was fuming at the thought of a fourth grader being better than she was at anything. Before Libby could tell Brittany about her new plan, Mim grabbed the baton and raced off down the gym.

Now Libby got into position to accept the baton and thought of the biggest reason why she hated relay races: It wasn't so much that she didn't like running—she just didn't like having to run fast. Mim turned and came speeding toward her. Suddenly the baton was being thrust into her hand and Libby became aware that her team was winning. Libby took off as fast as she could, but in four strides everyone flew by her as if they had the advantage of running on one of those moving walkways they have in the airport.

"Run!" Brittany screamed her lungs out and jumped up and down. Libby spun around and raced down the home stretch . . . when, to her horror, right before she was to pass the baton to Brittany . . . she dropped it! It hardly hit the floor when Brittany snatched it and rocketed to the far wall with lightning speed. In a flash she turned and was across the finish line past the others to win in spite of the slow-poke fumbler, Libby Thump.

TWEET! TWEET! The whistle blew.

Mrs. Whirly held Brittany's arm up and yelled out, "The winner!" even though technically Libby noted it wasn't just Brittany, it was the team. This was how it always was with Brittany. "Woo-hoo!" Brittany cried, and made a loud smack with her hands as she high-fived the teacher.

TWEET! The whistle echoed throughout the gym. Everyone settled down. "Remember, just like Brit here, we have to be *alert* and on our toes!" Mrs. Whirly said in her usual gung-ho gym-teacher voice. "*Wake up, girls!*"

Brittany beamed, and Libby wished she was her if only for this moment.

"What are we going to do, girls?" Mrs. Whirly cupped an ear and a smattering of kids half-heartedly mumbled, "Wake up."

"I can't hear you . . ." the gym teacher sang.

"*Wake up!*" the girls said together this time.

"Louder!" Mrs. Whirly yelled.

"*WAKE UP!*" everyone screamed.

The words reverberated inside Libby's head as she made her way to the locker room. Okay, it was just an expression like, "Go for it!" Mrs. Williams had said Libby didn't pay attention and Mr. Kaufman seemed to agree. Was Mrs. Whirly right? Did she need to be more alert and wake up?

One thing Libby knew as she watched the group of girls crowd around Brittany was that everybody loved a winner. Mrs. Whirly's voice called out, "You snooze, you lose, girls!"

Everything depended on Libby winning—possibly even the future of High Hopes Horse Farm. But for now she couldn't even get close enough to Brittany to explain her new idea. Instead Libby changed and headed to lunch, and vowed to herself that she would "wake up!"

It worked.

Right away she spotted Amanda sitting by herself. Again.

Libby slid into the seat next to Amanda, startling her. "Have you ever ridden in a horse show before?" Libby asked eagerly.

"Yes, lots," Amanda said confidently, "before we moved here."

"Did you ever win a blue ribbon?" Libby asked.

"Lots," the girl repeated.

"Okay, look, Sal needs our help," Libby said excitedly. "And I have the best idea!"

Amanda put her book down and listened.

"There's a horse show and if we can both go and win blue ribbons we can be Sal's star pupils, and he'll get lots of recognition and people will come back to High Hopes!"

Amanda nodded solemnly. "When is it?"

"In three weeks. Okay?" Libby nodded in encouragement.

"Okay," Amanda replied, and went back to eating her lunch.

"Great!" Libby was happy that Amanda said yes,

and thought she'd return the favor. Libby tried to be as diplomatic as possible. She spoke in a low voice now. "I guess you're new and everything . . . and don't take this the wrong way . . . but you know, you really shouldn't eat your lunch alone—the other kids will think you're weird."

"I know," Amanda said. "But I don't really care about other kids; all I care about is becoming a really good rider."

"Wow!" Libby said, surprised. "Really?" So that was it! Amanda was just trying to pay attention to her riding! "But you were able to get Cough Drop to jump. I think you're already pretty good."

"No." Amanda closed her eyes and shook her head. "I'm nowhere near as good as I hope I will be someday." She pushed her lunch away. "I mean, like, ten years from now—like internationally good."

Libby had absolutely no idea what she was talking about.

"Olympics," Amanda said impatiently. "Kids that

do gymnastics and skating start at my age. My mom says it takes a long time to get that good. My mom says that all I need to do is to just think about my riding." She glanced at Libby. "If I do, my mom says I'll have a head start."

Wow. Most of Libby's friends wanted stuff like a trip to Disneyland or an iPhone. Libby was impressed. Here Amanda was only ten years old and already thinking about the Olympics. "You snooze, you lose!" Libby exclaimed.

"Huh?" Amanda looked puzzled.

"Oh, nothing." Libby laughed and got up to leave. "It just something the gym teacher said that reminded me of you."

It seemed like such a coincidence that Mrs. Whirly's new expression fit Amanda so perfectly. *It's a sign!* Libby thought, and she went to her side of the lunchroom even more excited than before.

7

THE TROUBLE WITH SADDLESHOES

Libby hurried to the barn that very day after school more awake and alert than she'd ever been in her life. She rolled open Saddleshoes's stall door and the pony scowled at her. She tried to talk to him the way she always had Princess.

"Hi, Saddleshoes," she said in her nicest voice. The pony turned his hind end to her and gave her a dirty look. Libby continued, "I know you miss Kate, but—" Saddleshoes flattened his ears at her. "I, um, think you'll get to like me just as much, once you get to know me."

A bag of carrots later she was able to get him to come to the front of the stall, put on his halter, lead him to the aisle, and clip him to the cross ties. He nipped at her whenever she touched his sides with a brush. When she came anywhere near his hindquarters he switched his tail angrily at her.

Libby remained determined.

She inched up his girth little by little, the way Emily had shown her, and eased him out of the halter so that he wouldn't fly back and break another one. Then she took great care getting him into his bridle and suceeded after only the second try. She was even able to trot him for the first time, but every time she cantered him to the right he would pick up the left lead. "Wrong lead!" Emily called to Libby.

Libby had seen riders pull their horses' heads to the outside to get them to strike off on the inside leg at the canter. It wasn't the way you were supposed to do it.

Libby was desperate. She tried the technique, but even that didn't work!

"Wrong lead, Libby!" Emily called out again. "Just practice your trot."

Libby gritted her teeth. If she was ever going to win a blue ribbon she had to be able to canter on the correct lead. She wasn't going to ride in a walk-trot class with a bunch of eight-year-olds.

The next day was blustery and Libby sat on Saddleshoes, her knees gripped for dear life, while the pony shied every two minutes. "Just walk, Libby," Sal advised. Libby watched Brittany jump Summer. Brittany had started to learn to jump at the same time as Libby, but now she was easily going over a series of fences even higher than Libby had done on Princess. Amanda had come to the barn for the last two days as well and the entire place was buzzing about this new girl who could actually get Cough Drop to jump.

A horse whinnied in some far-off field and Saddleshoes's head went straight up. Libby held the reins even tighter and began to feel the raw spots on the insides of both of her knees. She couldn't help it. She did not want to fall off.

Every day that week Libby tried hard to ride the brown-and-white pony, but the trouble with Saddleshoes was that he was nothing like Princess. Just trotting a circle on this pony was hard and Libby felt like she was a beginner all over again. She had been at the barn longer than Brittany and she was older than Amanda but still doing baby stuff like "working at her trot." By Friday Libby still hadn't gotten him to canter on the correct lead. She was worried—the show was in two weeks.

On the other side of the ring Amanda aimed Cough Drop toward an in-and-out. Her mouth was set in a determined expression and her legs kicked as the pony balked. Before long they were through.

"Good job!" Emily clapped.

Libby left the ring and no one even noticed. Inside the barn it was quiet. She could see Sal through the door of his office, grimly hunched over his bills. As she walked down the aisle she passed by all the empty stalls. Libby worried what would happen if anyone else left. She silently untacked the pony and wiped off his back. Libby closed the stall door and leaned against it, completely demoralized. She felt bad for Sal but she felt worse for herself. She felt like she wanted to cry.

"Smile," a voice said.

Clip! Clop! Clip! Clop! It was the unmistakable sound of the giant horse, General George, echoing through the barn as his owner, Mr. McClave, led him down the aisle toward her.

Libby tried to smile but she thought her expression probably looked more like a grimace.

The old man's weathered face and white hair were visible under his cap. He had the bowed legs of a horseman and was dressed in his jeans with hacking boots and a jacket covered in horsehair. He clipped George to the cross ties. "So how's it going with Saddleshoes?"

Libby sat on a nearby tack trunk. "Not so hot."

He picked out a currycomb from his brush box and began to go over the enormous horse's neck in a circular motion. "I expect that pony is a lot different from riding Princess?"

Libby frowned. "All he does is shy and jig, Mr. McClave. His canter is impossible to sit to and he won't take the right lead. There's a show in two weeks and if I don't figure out how to ride him soon, everyone will be showing but me—and I've been here longer than all the other kids!"

"Doesn't seem fair, right, Libby?" Mr. McClave stopped to bang the currycomb against the side of a stall and a small cloud of dust and hair fell from it. Then he started currying the horse's other side. "Reminds me of the good old days when I first started riding this guy here." Mr. McClave tossed the currycomb into the grooming kit and took out a brush. He chuckled. "We had a lot of arguments back then."

"You did?" Libby said in a small voice.

He brushed the horse with long, sweeping strokes

as he talked. "He was four years old and wild in those days. He would take off across the fields with me and boy, oh boy, could he buck!"

Libby cocked her head and squinted her eyes, trying to imagine the bony, sleepy-eyed horse with his droopy lower lip in his younger days. "General George used to buck?"

Mr. McClave nodded. "Buck? He'd buck you to the moon when he was young!"

Libby sat up a little straighter to hear more. "Did you ever fall off?"

The old man laughed and waved a hand. "I fell off so many times the first year I rode him, I lost count!" He scratched George behind the ears and the horse lowered his head. "It was a battle—let me tell you—but now we're old war buddies, aren't we, boy?"

Libby scrunched up her nose. "What's a war buddy?"

Mr. McClave rested one hand on George's neck. The old man's shoulders were stooped and his voice was raspy with age, but his blue eyes twinkled as he recalled the past. "When you're in combat you're being tested every minute, Libby, just to stay alive. All you have are your buddies to watch your back and they're relying on you, too. These are the friendships that you never forget—the friends who were down in the trenches with you, fighting." He took a towel and went over the horse's coat. "This old war buddy of mine taught me a lot."

"Like what?" Libby asked.

"Well"—Mr. McClave stood back to inspect his grooming job on the horse—"patience, mostly, and how to listen." He turned to Libby and shook a finger at her. "It's very important, Libby, to learn to listen."

Libby thought if General George was as bad as Mr, McClave said, maybe there was hope for Saddleshoes. "How do you listen to a horse?"

Mr. McClave heaved a blue-and-white sheet expertly over the horse's back and leaned over to do up the buckles under George's belly. "You have to listen with your eyes and get to know his every move. You have to listen with your hands when you feel him on the other end of the reins or when you touch him. Listen with your legs to see how he responds to a squeeze when you ride him." The old man straightened stiffly and winked. "Listen to that pony, Libby, and you'll figure out how to ride him."

Libby hopped off the tack trunk and said good night to Mr. McClave.

She made her way down the aisle to Saddleshoes's stall and stood watching him. Maybe Mr. McClave was right. The pony stood sullenly at the back of the stall. She held out her hand. His nostrils flared as he sniffed her from his corner and then his ears flicked back and forth and went forward. For a second he actually looked like a nice pony.

"Good boy," Libby whispered. Maybe there was hope for her and Saddleshoes. She turned to go, feeling much better, and noticed at the end of the aisle a group that stood in front of the tack room in a discussion. As

Libby came closer she could hear their conversation.

Amanda stood with her chin pulled in a position that Libby had grown accustomed to seeing her take by now.

"Mom, why?" She held up a palm.

Her mother closed her eyes and shook her head. "No, Amanda, with the way you're riding right now you can't win—you need to practice more."

"She's riding well," Sal said surprised.

"Not well enough," her mother said.

Libby walked to the outside of the circle and listened.

Amanda pleaded, "Please, Mom—I know I can do really well."

"Well I don't, and I think I know better than you," her mother snapped.

Libby knew that if Project Blue Ribbons was ever going to work, Amanda *had* to get to that show. Libby had to do something!

Amanda's mother turned to leave. "I can't get you

here every day, Amanda, you know that—I have to work."

"Um, excuse me," Libby interrupted. "I have an idea."

Everyone turned to stare at her.

Libby stepped forward. "Why doesn't Amanda come with me after school and we can walk to the barn together?" Sal nodded as if he thought it was good idea, and Libby added, "Then she can have more practice and maybe go to the show."

Amanda beamed, "Please, Mom?"

"Well . . ." Her mother looked at Libby, unsure. "I'll have to speak to your mother. . . ."

"That's okay, she won't mind at all," Libby was quick to add. "It'll be fun."

Sal spoke. "I can vouch for Libby and her parents—Amanda will be fine."

So it was decided that three days a week Amanda could take the bus home with Libby, and they would both walk to the barn to ride. Libby was sure that

Amanda would get to the show. Brittany would make it there too. Now all Libby had to do was get herself and Saddleshoes there as well.

It was time to go home. Libby zipped up her jacket, but before she left for the night she went to check on Saddleshoes. He turned his head to look back at her and she was sure he was saying, *Go away*.

So much for listening. Libby knew there was a battle ahead.

8

LIBBY'S NEW BEST FRIEND

Two days later, according to plan, Amanda met Libby outside the school and together they rode the bus to her house. They stopped at Libby's for a snack and then changed into their riding clothes just as Libby's mother came in from a run. "Whew!" she said, and poured herself a glass of water.

"We jogged home from the bus today," Libby said proudly.

"You did?" Mrs. Thump was surprised. She was a

personal trainer at the gym and had tried to get Libby to go with her on her runs, but Libby never made it past the first block.

"Don't get too excited," Libby said. "Amanda's idea."

"Well done, Amanda," Mrs. Thump said, pleased. "And I hear you're a very good rider."

Amanda looked to Libby. "It's very nice of Libby to help me, thank you," she said politely.

"I'm sure Libby is thrilled to have another friend who loves horses as much as she does, right, honey?"

Libby nodded. She didn't mind having Amanda around. On the way home from the school bus she had made Libby jog with her because she'd heard that the really good riders jogged to get in shape. Libby had been out of breath by the second block but she had to admit it had been fun.

Mrs. Thump finished her water and turned to leave the room. "Would you like to come and have dinner with us on Sunday night, Amanda? Nothing fancy—just pizza or takeout?"

Libby was wondering what Amanda would say. She seemed so awkward at school, and Libby was surprised when she jumped at the offer. "Oh, I would love to come," she replied. Libby decided Amanda was one of those kids who felt more comfortable around adults.

As it turned out, Libby's mother was right. It was great to have a friend who was crazy about horses. Unlike Brittany, who Libby had always suspected rode only because Libby had found High Hopes Horse Farm first a year ago. Libby cringed just thinking about the day that Brittany had appeared last summer at Sal's—without even telling her—to ride, though she had never seemed to care about horses for as long as Libby had known her. Plus Brittany was good at everything: basketball, gymnastics, swimming; riding was just one more thing for her to be good at.

But Amanda was different. She didn't care about having a million friends or doing a hundred different sports. She didn't care about anything except horses. She wanted to grow up to be a really good rider. She was trying to live up to her potential—*just like me*, Libby thought.

It was fun for Libby to have someone she could teach everything there was to know about High Hopes Horse Farm to. Libby introduced Amanda to Mr. McClave and General George as well as to all of Sal's horses. She showed her where the tack sponges and saddle soap were kept, where the wheelbarrow, broom, and shovel were to sweep up after Cough Drop, and how to use the hose in the wash stall. Brittany had never cared about things like that. She just seemed to show up to ride and then left.

There was no doubt that Amanda was a "good little rider," as she'd heard Sal say. As far as Libby was concerned she was a really good rider and made the fat school pony, Cough Drop, look like a million bucks.

Libby figured that Brittany had noticed too but if she had, she never mentioned it. At school on Friday she passed Libby a note in Mr. Kaufman's class.

It said: *Want to go shopping with me and my mom on Saturday?*

Libby had loved to go shopping with Brittany and her mom. They always went to the best stores, the kind that had a café where they could have lunch. It had always been fun . . . until now.

Libby shook her head no.

Brittany tilted hers and mouthed, *Why not?*

Libby wrote back, *Hoping Sal lets me ride in the show next weekend—need to practice!!!*

Brittany pursed her lips when she read it and scribbled back: *Riding with that dorky Amanda???*

Libby made a face at Brittany, but her best friend had guessed right—Libby *had* made plans to ride with Amanda all weekend. Libby remembered guiltily that she still hadn't told Brittany about her plan for them all to win blue ribbons at the show and help Sal attract more students and boarders. But why should she? Brittany would win anyway—she always did at everything she tried.

Libby glanced at Brittany and the other girl looked away. She *had* been truthful, though, she *did* need to practice, Libby thought defensively, and she chewed nervously on the tip of her pen. At the rate she was riding Saddleshoes, both Amanda and Brittany would be going to the show and jumping and Libby would be stuck in the walk-trot class with a bunch of the eight-year-old riders.

There was even the awful possibility that she wouldn't get to go at all. Sal hadn't mentioned it. Emily only noticed enough to say, "Wrong lead, Libby," or "Just walk for now, Libby." When all the other kids went out on the trails Sal said, "Stay in the ring, Libby. Don't take Saddleshoes out unless I'm with you, Libby," but Sal was hardly ever around anymore. He was always in his office in front of his computer or else on his cell phone. It seemed like he had a thundercloud over his head.

Libby heard Sal and Emily talking all the time.

"Things will improve by summer," Emily had said to Sal.

"We can't wait till summer, Emily—we need more boarders now," Libby heard Sal reply.

Friday night Libby wrote in her notebook:

PROJECT BLUE RIBBON

Wake up! One week to
horse show!
Live up to your potential!!!! For
High Hopes Horse Farm!

When Libby got on Saddleshoes that Saturday it looked as though it could rain any minute, and Libby could understand why many of the boarders had chosen to leave Sal's in favor of the comfort of an indoor ring. She looked at the barn door and wished that Sal would come out and give her a lesson.

Now it was just her and Brittany.

Libby rode up next to the other girl. "Has Sal told you if you're riding in the show next weekend?"

"Yes, he said I could go," she said a little coolly.

Libby bit her lip. "He hasn't said a word to me yet."

Brittany tossed her head and changed the subject. "I thought you'd be riding with *Amanda* today."

Even though they had planned to ride together at

the last minute, Amanda had come early and taken a lesson. Libby shook her head. Sal had told Brittany she could go to the show but he hadn't told Libby—that wasn't good.

Brittany picked up on Libby's worried mood. "Well you still have a week to get to the show. Come on," she said when Libby didn't answer. "Let's get out of this ring and go on the trails—we'll just walk."

Sal had told Libby she wasn't ready to leave the ring yet with Saddleshoes. "I'm not allowed," Libby said.

"Oh, come on," Brittany persisted.

"I'm really not supposed to," Libby protested, but she suddenly thought of how impressed Sal would be if she *did* take Saddleshoes out of the ring. That would be progress!

"We'll only go down the driveway—no farther," Brittany said persuasively. "If Shoes acts up, we'll just turn back. Come on."

"All right." Libby pushed back her shoulders and shortened her reins.

They walked side by side out through the gate, and Libby thought that maybe now she would tell Brittany about Project Blue Ribbons when Brittany turned to Libby. "I just can't *believe* you're bringing that Amanda kid with you after school to the barn."

"Her mom has to work and I just wanted to help her out," Libby said.

Brittany scrunched up her nose.

"What?" Libby said.

"I don't know, she's such a little weirdo," Brittany complained.

"She's okay." Libby knew Amanda was different but she liked her. "You should give her a chance, Brit."

Brittany made a face, and that's when it happened: Saddleshoes dropped his shoulder and jumped to the side. He wheeled and suddenly they were facing the other direction. Before she could get her balance he took off with her back to the barn. She righted herself and stood up in the stirrups to lean her entire weight against the reins but he only went faster. The pony got his head down, rounded his back, and bucked once . . . twice . . . She was going to fall! She knew she was going to fall! Even as she flew through the air and braced herself for the impact, she couldn't believe it was really happening. The ground was coming toward her at a terrible speed. *CRASH!* She landed her full weight on her side.

She scrambled onto her knees and saw the back of the brown-and-white pony, his stirrups banging at his sides as if an invisible rider were urging him on. Brittany came galloping up on Summer. Saddleshoes had raced into the barn and Sal and Emily came running.

"Are you okay?" Brittany had reached her and jumped off Summer.

"Libby, are you all right?" Sal and Emily were both talking at the same time

"I'm fine, I'm *fine*!" Libby brushed dirt off her pants.

"Why did you leave the ring?" Sal asked after he could see she was all right.

"I'm sorry, Sal," Libby mumbled. "I just thought

if I could bring him out of the ring you'd . . ."

Brittany tried to explain. "We just walked up the driveway, that's all."

Sal frowned and shook his head.

"Are you really all right?" Brittany whispered to her as they walked back to the barn.

"Yes," Libby said impatiently, but she really wasn't so sure. She'd landed right on her arm and she could feel it throbbing now. She immediately went to the tack room and took off her jacket to inspect it, when Mr. McClave walked in.

"What happened?" he said, surprised.

"I fell off," Libby said, annoyed. The old man looked at her elbow, which was scraped up.

"Didn't hit your head now, did you?" he asked.

"No." That much she was sure of—besides, she'd had on her riding helmet.

"Can you move your arm?" the old man asked calmly.

Libby bent it a few times. "Yes."

"Long as you can move it—it's all right," he proclaimed. "Just a war wound, my girl. You should be proud of your battle scars! Hurt in the line of duty!"

Libby smiled weakly. She wasn't so sure.

9

WAR BUDDIES

Sal had insisted on driving Libby home, and the entire way she tried to think of how *not* to tell anyone what had happened. But that plan went right out the window because Sal insisted on coming inside to tell her mother.

Soon the whole family was gathered around. Her father examined her arm. Her sister was impressed. "So when you slammed into the ground like a ton of bricks, what did it feel like?"

"Laurel, that's enough," Mrs. Thump said. The next thing Libby knew she was on her way to the emergency room. Libby sat waiting for the results of her X-ray thinking about all that had happened. So many things had gone wrong lately that she was caught completely by surprise to hear that her arm was just badly bruised.

"But no pony riding for the next few days, young lady," the doctor said.

Pony riding? She could always tell the people who'd never been near a horse in their lives. "Pony riding" made it sound like she was at some little kid's birthday party or the county fair.

The next day was Sunday, and Libby got to stay in her pajamas and watch TV all morning but she couldn't help feeling anxious about what Saddleshoes would be like in a couple of days, having not been ridden.

Around noontime she was restless and asked her mother, "What if I just go over and get on him for twenty minutes?"

"*N. O.* No!" her mother said. "I don't like the idea of you riding that pony at all anymore. I'm going to talk to Sal!"

"No! Mom!" Libby said angrily.

Sal had given her the pony because he had thought she would be able to handle him. Now the minute she falls off she goes crying to her mother? Libby couldn't stand the thought of that. She wasn't a quitter!

"Mom, please just give me a few more weeks, please?" Libby could see her mother was worried and tried to reassure her. "I know it'll be all right," she said.

Her mother didn't answer, but she didn't say no, either.

That night Amanda showed up at the door with the stern face that Libby thought probably was also her concerned face. Her arms were across her chest. Her chin retracted. "Are you okay?" she said in a hushed voice.

"I'm fine, fine, fine!" Libby was getting tired of everyone asking.

Libby's father came home with Chinese takeout and soon they were all in the family room.

"This is the best Chinese food I've ever had!" Amanda ate like it was her last meal. Libby was pleasantly surprised by Laurel, who was being nice for a change, and offered to get Amanda a second helping, but the younger girl jumped out of her seat and got it herself.

"Let's go to my room," Libby said after dinner. That's what she and Brittany and Mim always did whenever they ate at each other's house. But Amanda cleared the dishes, helped put them in the dishwasher, and talked a blue streak with Libby's mother—which confirmed Libby's theory that Amanda was indeed one of those kids that got along better with adults.

"You're very grown up for your age," Mrs. Thump remarked, and laughed. "I can never get Libby to hang around and clean up the kitchen!"

"Thank you, Mrs. Thump," Amanda said, and rearranged the glasses in the dishwasher.

"But you're our guest tonight, Amanda—you don't have to do all this!" Mrs. Thump said.

"Oh, I do this every night at home—it's just a habit," Amanda said capably.

Libby couldn't help thinking it was a good thing that Brittany wasn't here right now—she could just hear her comparing Amanda to that kid in their class who sat up front and always asked for more homework to the groans of the entire class.

"Well, not tonight." Mrs. Thump shook a dish towel at Amanda. "Go have fun. I can do the rest here."

The girls headed to Libby's room with Margaret padding right behind.

"You're so lucky," Amanda said wistfully.

Libby rubbed her aching arm. She didn't exactly feel lucky right then. "Lucky—why?"

"I don't know," Amanda said dully.

Margaret jumped onto Libby's bed and rolled over on her back for a belly rub. Amanda sat on the bed as well and petted the dog, but she'd become subdued.

"What's wrong?" Libby asked.

Amanda frowned. "My mom is still against me showing Cough Drop next week."

"Why?" Libby didn't understand. Amanda was riding so well, Libby was sure she'd win at the show.

Amanda flopped on one side, an elbow supporting her. "She doesn't think Cough Drop is a good enough pony to win on, and she's not happy unless I win. It's driving me nuts!"

"My mom is driving me nuts too," Libby said sympathetically. "She doesn't want me to ride Saddleshoes anymore."

"Oh no!" Amanda sat up.

Libby picked at the bedspread. "She's just afraid that I'll get hurt."

Amanda nodded knowingly. "I just wish I was grown up."

"Me too!" Libby agreed.

Libby looked at her arm again. It had turned green

and yellow and purple and was swollen. "It doesn't look too bad, does it?"

Amanda craned her neck to see over Margaret, who was between them. It seemed like she didn't know what to say.

"Mr. McClave called it a battle scar." Libby poked at her arm to see if it still hurt. It did.

"I like that." Amanda grinned.

"A battle scar in the War of the Saddleshoes!" Libby said in a deep voice, and both girls laughed.

Libby turned serious again. "I'm not allowed to ride for a few days, though—which is ridiculous—Shoes is going to be a maniac by the time I get on him again."

Amanda sat up. "Do you want me to ride him for you?"

"You're not afraid?" Libby asked.

"No!" Amanda was sure.

"It's okay with me if it's okay with Sal," Libby said. "Thanks—thanks a lot."

It was getting late and Amanda stood. "Nobody's ever been so nice to me, Libby."

"That's how friends are," Libby said. "Mr. McClave says that in war your friends are the ones who have your back. He called them war buddies."

"We both have a battle ahead, that's for sure," Amanda said softly.

Libby's face lit up. "I know! When we grow up we'll *both* try out for the equestrian team and go to the Olympics! And we'll have each other's back," Libby said, and held out her hand to shake. "Deal?"

Amanda nodded. "Deal," she said, and they shook on it.

10

HORSE SHOW JITTERS

"Mom, can't I just go to the barn for twenty minutes?" Libby pleaded again Monday afternoon.

"*N.O.* No," her mother said again. "It won't be the end of the world if you take a few days off."

The weather was warm and bright, but Libby was stuck at home. She could barely concentrate on her homework thinking that her last week to impress Sal to let her ride in the show was slipping through her fingers.

• • •

Libby looked for Amanda at lunch on Tuesday but the table where the lone fourth grader usually sat was empty. Where was she? Had something happened when she rode Saddleshoes? Libby began to imagine every awful scenario. What if he bit Amanda when she tried to do up his girth? What if he ran away with her? Or bucked her off? That night Libby phoned Amanda's house several times but there was no answer. What was going on?

On Wednesday Libby finally found Amanda waiting outside the school. "Are you *all right*?" Libby tried to keep the anxiety out of her voice.

"Everything is fine!" Amanda reassured her. Just then her mother drove up and honked the horn loudly. Amanda went to leave.

"How's Saddleshoes?" Libby called.

"He's fine—I'm headed there to ride him now!" Amanda jumped in the car. "Don't worry!"

But Libby did worry. That afternoon she wrote miserably in her notebook:

Project Blue Ribbons: On hold until further notice.

She sat in her bedroom and stewed. Margaret sighed. She curled up, stared into space, and stewed along with her. Libby absently stroked the dog's back with one hand. "Amanda is such a good rider. Is it because she started when she was three?" Margaret's tail wagged a few times and Libby took that as a yes. "Or maybe it's because riding just comes easier to her . . . than it does to me?" The dog rolled over onto her back. "You're no help, Margaret," Libby said glumly.

She lay on her side and absently rubbed the dog's belly, thinking. What was going on at High Hopes Horse Farm right now? Was Saddleshoes behaving better for Amanda than he had for her? In an instant the image of the pony bucking Amanda off came to Libby and she had to admit it made her happy for a second, but then she thought, *Amanda and I are "war buddies." We have each other's back. Don't we?*

Libby sat in Mr. Kaufman's class the next day convinced that Amanda was a better rider than she was probably because she paid better attention instead of stewing over things all the time the way Libby did. She glanced at the clock again, counting the minutes till lunch so that she could find Amanda, when Brittany slipped a crumpled-up piece of paper onto Libby's desk. Libby furtively opened it on her lap. It said: *News flash! Amanda is BUTTING in on SADDLESHOES!!!! The show is Sunday—you have to come back to the barn to ride TODAY!!!!!!!*

"It's okay," Libby said to Brittany after class. They walked down the hallway, weaving in and out of the throngs of kids. Libby looked for Amanda but she was nowhere to be seen.

"Okay?" Brittany said with disbelief. "She's been riding him every day that you've been gone!"

"I told her—no, asked her—to ride him, Brittany,"

Libby tried to explain. "Someone's got to otherwise he'll be totally impossible to ride by the time I get back. She's helping me."

Brittany huffed, "I thought her mother was *soooooo* busy that Amanda had to come home with *you* to get to the barn every day. Doesn't look like she's having any problem *now*."

"Look, I don't know," Libby said lightly. She had wondered that as well but she figured Amanda's mom probably just wanted to help out too.

Brittany pushed the air away with a hand. "Sal is supposed to post the schedule for the show on Saturday. You'd better come back or else Amanda will be riding Saddleshoes."

"That's crazy, Brittany!" Libby knew Amanda wasn't going to do that. Brittany was just being her old competitive self.

Brittany tossed her head and turned to walk away. "All right—but don't say I didn't warn you."

Libby watched Brittany disappear into the crowd.

"What's wrong with her?" Mim had joined up with Libby.

"It's just Brittany. She's all upset because Amanda has been riding Saddleshoes while I'm not there."

Mim understood completely without any further explanation. She'd known Brittany all her life, just like Libby. "She's probably just jittery about the show."

Both girls laughed because they knew there was no way Brittany was going to tolerate a fourth grader out-riding her. But when Libby entered the lunchroom and saw the empty table where Amanda always sat, Libby had an uneasy feeling that she did need to get back to the barn—today.

"Remember—no riding yet!" her mother called as Libby raced out the door.

"I promise!" Libby called back. She ran all the way. Princess came running as soon as she saw the girl coming over the top of the hill. Libby hugged the horse's neck. Then she rolled up the sleeve of her shirt and held out her arm with the deep purple bruise that now reached almost to her wrist. Princess sniffed it loudly. Libby fed her a carrot. "I wish we could go back to the way things were," Libby said softly. "I just don't know if I'm ever going to learn how to ride that pony. . . . Maybe I'm just not good enough."

The mare shook her head and followed Libby down the hill the way she always did when Libby used to ride her. At the gate Libby straightened Princess's forelock, said good-bye, and made her way to the ring. She picked the same place to stand, in the shadows at the far corner, under the same tree as Amanda had a few weeks before. The longer Libby stood there the more she had the strangest feeling, as if she and Amanda had somehow exchanged places. Now Libby was the outsider who watched the girl jump fences as her pigtails flew in the wind behind her.

"Turn right and come over the gate," Sal called out.

Saddleshoes pricked his ears and for a second it looked like he might try to run out, but Amanda caught him just in time and he jumped.

"Good job!" Sal yelled happily. "Now turn and take the in-and-out then the barrels!" Emily, Amanda's mother, and even Mr. McClave stood in the middle watching with delight. Amanda's eyes were fixed on the line to the two fences. She sat a little farther back and her legs urged him. His head came up and she kept her hands down and steady. Then she turned across the ring to the barrels, which were standing on their ends. It was a good-size jump—the biggest Libby had ever seen the pony take, even with Kate. He shot forward as soon as he saw the fence, and Libby's heart was in her throat because he was going too fast. He sprang off the ground with room to spare. Everyone cheered.

Libby could feel the bitter sting of tears behind her eyes. It was plain as day that Saddleshoes went better for Amanda than he did for her. She didn't want anyone to see her but it was too late, Brittany had been in the ring as well and was coming toward her. "I told you," she said out of the side of her mouth.

Libby shook her head. "It's not Amanda's fault.

She's just a really good rider—and I stink."

"You do *not*, Libby!" Brittany said vehemently.

"Yes. I do," Libby insisted, and walked toward the barn with Brittany alongside her.

"Don't say that, Libby—you're a good rider!" Brittany said angrily.

Libby turned to go but Brittany stopped her. "Wait! Come with me to the barn—Sal just said that he posted the schedule for the show on Sunday."

The show! Libby didn't know what would be worse: to be in it and riding in the embarrassing walk-trot, or to be riding in some class where she had to canter around on the wrong lead. Minutes later the two girls stood before the list. Everyone was going to the show but Libby. She'd never felt so relieved or so awful at the same time before.

Brittany gave her a worried look. "You're coming to the show anyway, though, right?"

"Wrong," Libby said.

"You have to come for moral support!" Brittany moaned.

Libby turned to leave.

Brittany grabbed her jacket. "Look!" She pointed to the last class of the day. "See that?"

Libby could see that Brittany and Amanda were in the same class together. It was equitation under twelve with the fences at two feet six inches.

"Please come, Libby. Please," Brittany pleaded.

Before Libby could answer they both saw Amanda leading Saddleshoes. Brittany took Summer to her stall. "Remember, Libby—you're going to the horse show Sunday."

Amanda was smiling from ear to ear. Her cheeks were rosy from exertion. She seemed genuinely happy to see Libby. "Yay! You're back!" she called to her.

"You did really well with him." Libby tried to keep the hurt out of voice. In the few days that she'd been away, obviously Saddleshoes had forgotten all about her.

"He's not easy." Amanda pulled off her helmet and her hair was sweaty underneath. "Saddleshoes bolted and I could barely stop him the first day. I nearly got run away with the first two days. I can see why you've had so much trouble. But I have a secret," she said mischievously.

"What?" Libby asked.

Amanda pointed to the pony's mouth. "New bit!" she said triumphantly.

Sure enough, Libby could see in place of the snaffle was a different bit with a curb chain that went under his chin.

"It's called a Kimberwick. They used them all the time back where I used to ride. Sal said it was all right so I tried it!"

"That's great, Amanda," Libby said, and suddenly Saddleshoes stretched out his neck and sniffed Libby's hand. Amanda pulled him away.

"Amanda!" her mother yelled. She stood with Sal in front of the tack room where they had been talking. "Hurry up, we have to go!"

Amanda quickly led the pony to his stall.

Libby looked with amazement at the hand Saddleshoes had sniffed. Had the pony remembered her after all? Was it possible?

11
HORSE SHOW

Sunday morning Libby woke with a start. Margaret had burrowed under the covers sometime during the night and was pressed warmly against Libby's legs. The image of Amanda jumping Saddleshoes over the barrels bubbled to the surface of her consciousness and Libby groaned. She threw back the covers and got out of bed.

She wasn't riding but Amanda and Brittany were. Maybe they both would win blue ribbons for High

Hopes Horse Farm and bring some people back to Sal's. She had to get to the show. Project Blue Ribbons could still work!

When she got downstairs she could hear her mother moving about the kitchen, making breakfast, and the familiar sound of her sister, Laurel, complaining.

"But why not?" she cried. She was fifteen and seemed to say this a lot. Libby remembered the time Laurel wanted to get a tattoo. "Why not?" she had wailed. Then there was the other time she had carried on so about coloring her hair pink. "Why not?" It was the same when she wanted to wear false eyelashes. Libby drank her juice and made toast while Laurel once again argued her point.

"But *why not,* Mom?" she said, and her mouth hung open in utter bewilderment that her mother couldn't seem to understand. "I already *wore* that to the last dance—everybody has *seen* it."

Libby's mother sipped her coffee and gazed at Laurel over the edge of her cup, unmoved. "Well, how about your yellow dress—the one with the cute little white collar?"

Laurel put her head down on the table in despair. Her voice came from the crook of her elbow in a sort of muffled sob. "From seventh grade? Yeah right."

Libby figured this was a good place to interrupt. "Um, could someone please take me to the horse show?"

Libby's father had been eating a plate of eggs. He scooped up the last forkful and slid out of his seat. "I'll go."

Libby's mom raised her eyebrows. "You mean you don't want to stay here and try to convince Laurel why she doesn't need yet another new dress for yet another dance?"

"Not really," he said breezily. Mr. Thump kissed his wife on the cheek and Laurel glared at both of them.

Libby sat in the front seat and Margaret was in the back with her head hanging over the armrest.

"Phew!" Her father said. "Glad I'm outta there!" He stopped at a light and turned to Libby, "So how's the arm—I'll bet you're chomping at the bit to get back to riding."

"Yes, I am!" Libby agreed, and they both laughed at his lame joke.

They started down the street again and her father turned more serious. "Your mother and I are so proud of you, Libby." His face looked tense. "I just wish we could get you your own horse."

Libby knew they couldn't afford it. Her mother worked at the gym and her father had his own landscaping business—until last fall. After having his own business his entire life, he had taken a job working for someone else. Libby said cheerfully, "How is it going at work?"

Her father kept his eyes on the road. "It's an adjustment."

Libby looked out the window. They were traveling through what used to be acres and acres of farmland, which was being sold off, and in its place gigantic houses had started to crop up. They passed a golf course just like the one her father managed now and

Libby was suddenly glad that she was still a kid. "Is it hard—I mean, the new job?"

Mr. Thump laughed softly. "It's just change, Lib. None of us likes it—but things are constantly changing and we all have to adapt—including me."

Change, Libby thought. *Like not being able to ride Princess anymore.* She knew exactly what her father was talking about. "Anyway, it's okay, Dad, this pony I'm riding now is practically like my own."

"You know, Libby, you're lucky that you've found something you love to do—besides shopping. I wish your sister was more like that."

Libby stared at her feet with Laurel's riding boots. Laurel had given them to Libby when she stopped riding because she was more interested in boys and her social life. Libby knew that would never be her—she would never stop riding because she was more interested in boys!

"It's just nice that you've found something you're really good at," her father said.

"I'm not *that* good, Dad," Libby said quietly.

"You will be someday," he said.

Lately Libby wasn't so sure. They pulled into the farm where the show was. "I'll just get a ride back to the barn with Sal," Libby said, and waved good-bye.

"Are you sure you don't want to come home earlier— you know, since you're not riding?" her father asked.

Libby shook her head. Maybe she could even talk about High Hopes to other riders . . . maybe she could still help Sal. But as she headed through a field all by herself to where the trailers were parked, she began to feel blue, like it was a mistake to come here at all this morning. She had been the first one to start riding at High Hopes Horse Farm. She had cleaned up Princess when Sal had all but forgotten about the big white mare. Now here Libby was all but forgotten, passed by the way she had been in the relay race at school . . . like she was standing still.

No. It wasn't fair.

Libby went looking for Brittany and found Sal's van

right away, but no one was around. Sal had been right; it was a small show but the air still buzzed with nervous energy. She headed to the ring to see if Brittany was there. The smell of coffee and bacon frying came from a food truck. Little girls with colorful ribbons at the ends of their braids bounced by on small ponies that looked like wind-up toys. Mothers stood holding all kinds of gear: jackets, buckets filled with brushes, riding helmets, gloves, crops. There was Emily schooling her horse, Benson, in an open sand arena.

"Libby!" she called. Emily needed her to set up some fences. Libby was happy to have something to do. For twenty minutes she stood in the center putting up rails. But when Emily headed off for her class Libby sighed. It really wasn't any fun being at a show unless she was riding. Plus what was she going to do, walk up to people and say, "Hi, you should come to High Hopes Horse Farm. It's a great place to ride just because?" *It was a stupid idea*, Libby thought and wished again she'd stayed at home when she heard a shout.

"Hey, um, kid—could you help me?" a voice said.

Libby turned to see a man on a large bay horse with a braided mane. He was probably the skinniest guy she'd ever seen. He looked like a scarecrow with his bony knees that were visible from inside his breeches and his wrists that poked out of his black riding jacket. His ears stuck out from either side of his riding helmet and he wore glasses, but as improbable as it was, he looked terrific on a horse. Was he talking to her? Libby pointed to herself. *Me?*

He nodded and waved her over and mumbled a question to her. "What?" Libby asked.

"Could you—I mean . . . Would you, like, for a second, raise that rail?" He had a shy, crooked smile and now Libby could see that he was more of an older boy than a man.

"Sure!" Libby said. Pretty soon she was building fences and putting up rails when he knocked them down like she had for Emily. Libby could tell this guy was a really good rider. She squinted into the sun and watched him approach a high single rail fence. His horse's mouth was white with foam. He came in at

a collected bouncy canter. "Wait . . . wait," she could hear the rider say gently to his horse, who he checked one . . . two strides, and then pushed him the last stride. The horse sprang over the fence like a deer, hovered in the air a split second, and then they landed.

He pulled up in front of Libby and flashed her his lopsided grin. "Thanks! You're the best fence-putter-upper, or whatever, I've ever seen," he teased. "Where'd you learn to do that?"

"Oh, I help Emily all the time over at High Hopes Horse Farm," Libby said.

"Emily?" he asked.

"Emily Ricci—she's married to Sal?"

"Oh yeah, I remember him." He nodded. "I've been kind of out of the loop for a while, but, hey—do they—they wouldn't have any, like, room over there, would they?"

"You mean, stalls?" Libby couldn't believe what she was hearing.

"Yeah, I can't afford the place I'm at now." He

talked like he had marbles in his mouth but Libby could tell he was embarrassed.

"Really? That's great! I mean, you need to talk to Sal right now!" Libby looked around to see if he was anywhere near. "What's your name?"

"Ian—I can't, like, talk to him *right* now; I'm in this class right after the kids' equitation—"

Kids' equitation? That was Brittany and Amanda! Libby had almost completely forgotten all about it. "Gosh! I have to go!" she yelled over her shoulder. "Talk to Sal—he's around here somewhere!" Libby ran all the way to the ring and squeezed in between the moms just in time to watch Amanda go over the first fence. It was perfection. Well, as perfect as Cough Drop could be. He puffed all the way around and heaved himself up over the fences, but Amanda's form was excellent. As they left the ring there was no denying that she was one of the best young riders at the show. Her mother appeared from the crowd and elbowed people out of the way. Holding her phone, she snapped pictures of her daughter like crazy.

Libby waited for Brittany and just when she thought she might have missed her, Summer appeared at the gate. They were the last to ride in the class. Libby could see why. Summer's head was straight up in the air and her neck was lathered with sweat. She was upset and nervous—just the way she'd been when Laurel took her to a show last summer. Brittany had probably been trying to calm the mare down all this time.

Brittany's face was white and her eyes were wide as she circled at the top of the ring. Sal and Emily stood at the gate looking concerned as they watched. Summer came into the first fence weaving and looking everywhere but at the jump. It seemed like she would stop but then at the last minute she leaped off the ground with all four feet in the air at once and almost unseated her rider. To Brittany's credit she brought the horse back to a trot, but Summer tried to run out of the next fence. Brittany kept her from doing that but then the horse jumped at the last minute.

There was an audible gasp from the mothers standing by Libby. Rails went flying in every direction; Brittany teetered to one side and almost fell off for the second time. She looked completely rattled as she made the turn and Summer did duck out of the third fence. When they came around for a second try, Summer stopped at the fence.

Brittany tried to pull herself together. She gathered her reins and approached the jump again, but her horse was having none of it. She stopped a third time.

"Thank you!" the judges called. Brittany and Summer had been eliminated.

Brittany left the ring. Libby was about to leave as well to console her friend but she stayed for a moment to see who had won. A few minutes later a smiling Amanda trotted Cough Drop in to accept her blue ribbon. Her mom stood at the gate, her phone held at eye level, most likely videotaping her daughter.

Libby hurried around the ring to congratulate Amanda and ran into Brittany.

Summer now looked annoyingly calm, as if she knew she was done for the day and could go home. Brittany on the other hand was smoldering with anger.

"Sorry—" Libby tried to speak to her.

"Yeah, right," Brittany said without stopping. "Thanks—thanks a lot."

Libby stood motionless, not knowing what to do or say. She felt bad now that she hadn't been able to at least wish her friend good luck before her class. But how was she supposed to know that Brittany had been relying on her so much? Brittany was always so self-assured. Libby never dreamed Brittany needed anyone!

Libby started off after Brittany to see if she could talk to her, when she spotted Amanda, who stood just outside the ring posing next to Cough Drop while her mom took pictures. Amanda looked just like a real show rider dressed in her fitted jacket, breeches, and boots, holding the pony with the blue ribbon that fluttered off his bridle. Libby was so proud to be friends with this girl!

"Congratulations, Amanda!" Libby called, but Amanda was busy with Sal and Emily.

It was so exciting and Libby knew Amanda must be so happy. Libby waited until Sal and Emily were finished congratulating Amanda and then rushed to her to do the same. "Congratulations, Amanda!" Libby exclaimed again.

Amanda was putting her stirrups up and only glanced at Libby for a second. "What?"

"You rode so well!" Libby touched the blue ribbon. It was as beautiful as she imagined. She watched as Amanda pushed the flap of the saddle up so that she could loosen the girth. "Here, I'll hold him." Libby took the pony's reins helpfully. "Cough Drop looked amazing!" Libby said, impressed.

"I was pleased," Amanda replied.

Libby gave the pony a few good pats on his neck. "I wish I could have ridden Saddleshoes today. Wouldn't it have been great if we had *both* won blue ribbons?"

Amanda was preoccupied with the billet straps on

the saddle and once again didn't seem to hear Libby.

"It would've been so cool—I mean if we'd both won. Wouldn't it?" Libby said again.

"Libby!" Amanda's mother stood a few feet in front of them with her phone poised to take another picture. She waved her arm for Libby to get out of the way.

"Oh! Sorry!" Libby handed Amanda the reins and scrambled off to the side.

Amanda's mother took a few more pictures and hurried her daughter away.

It would *have been so cool if we'd both won blue ribbons today,* Libby thought wistfully as she watched them go.

12

NEW HORSES AT HIGH HOPES

That Monday it was a chilly day outside for the end of May but it was just as cold in the cafeteria at Libby's school. Brittany sat clear across the room at another table, eating her lunch.

Mim sat with Libby, her sandwich untouched. She had her hair pulled up into a bun with a pink ribbon around it. It was ballet-lesson day. Nice, safe, ballet-lesson day, where you didn't have too far to fall, Libby thought, and tried to remember why she had never liked the ballet classes that her mother had made her take when she was eight. Oh yeah, that's right—she was awful at ballet.

"We've been sitting together since first grade," Mim said, baffled by Brittany's sudden departure to the other side of the room.

Libby leaned on one elbow, her chin in her hand. She'd become so caught up in congratulating Amanda at the show that she'd completely forgotten to talk to Brittany. By the time she'd gotten back to Sal's van, Brittany had gone. "Amanda beat Brittany at the horse show yesterday."

"No! Really?" Mim couldn't believe it. Very few kids ever beat Brittany at anything.

"Her horse, Summer, was terrible," Libby said.

"But that's not *our* fault." Mim bit into her sandwich.

No, it wasn't their fault, Libby thought. It also wasn't *her* fault either that she'd gotten sidetracked by first Emily and then Ian at the show and hadn't been able to help Brittany before her class. She'd never seen Brittany lose . . . at anything. Maybe Brittany just needed someone to be angry with and to blame right now. *She's just mad that she lost and is taking it out on me,* Libby thought.

"So what are you going to do?" Mim asked.

Libby shrugged. Brittany always came to the barn on Mondays and Libby hoped that after she rode she would be in a better mood.

Mim put her sandwich down and stared over Libby's shoulder. "Don't look now," Mim said in a low voice, "but I think we are about to have a new lunchmate."

It was Amanda. She was walking quickly toward them in that erect, stiff way of hers, balancing a sandwich on top of a crumpled piece of tin foil. Libby and Mim moved over to make more room and she took the seat next to Libby.

Mim immediately congratulated Amanda. "Libby said you did really well on Saturday."

Amanda's cheeks were flushed. "Thanks," she said brusquely, and turned to Libby. "You missed it!"

"Missed what?" Libby asked.

"Ian!" Amanda was all agog with the big news. "He brought his two horses to the barn after the show, and he's the most fantastic rider, and he's going to board and—and you should see him ride!"

Libby was thrilled. Having two more horses at High Hopes would definitely help Sal. "I *have* seen him ride!" Libby said. "At the show—I set up fences for him and he said he needed a place to board his horses, so I told him about the barn." Libby thought that Amanda would be impressed that she had been the one to tell Ian about High Hopes.

She was a little disappointed when Amanda hadn't seemed to hear, though. "My mom can't take me to the barn today—can I come with you?" she said with a desperate little smile.

"Sure," Libby said. She pointed her thumb at the empty seat next to her. "I guess you can tell that Brittany is a little upset."

Amanda hadn't noticed. "She is? Why?"

"She doesn't like to lose, that's all," Mim said, joining the conversation.

Amanda frowned for a second, then suddenly her

eyes grew large. "Oh my gosh! There's something else." The subject of Brittany was quickly forgotten and Libby marveled at Amanda for not being the least bit caught up in the aura of Brittany's awesomeness. "Ian said—"

"You talked to him?" Libby was all ears.

"Yes." Amanda's eyes were bright with excitement. "He said that in a few weeks there's another show—it's on June twenty-first!"

"That's the first day of summer!" Libby said, excited now as well. School would be out by then and she would have the two entire months to ride at High Hopes. What better way to start it than with a horse show? She would have another chance. Libby couldn't wait to write it down in her notebook.

That afternoon Libby and Amanda raced to the barn to find Sal, Emily, and Mr. McClave standing in a little group, peering into a stall. Sal looked like he was in a better mood. "I met Ian at the show on Saturday!" Libby said proudly.

Sal hadn't seemed to hear her. He opened the stall

door to the bay horse. "Did you see this one, Mr. M?"

"They're both the best-looking horses I've seen in a long time," Mr. McClave said.

"And he's one of the best riders I've seen in a long time," Emily added.

"He remembered Princess from our glory days. Said he'd never seen such a great mare," Sal said proudly, and closed the stall door.

"It's so mysterious, though." Emily shook her head. "I heard that Ian had been picked for a training session with the equestrian team and never showed up—no one knows why."

"Probably both his horses went lame?" Sal speculated.

"No, I heard he just never showed up." Emily held out her arms and let them drop. "He disappeared right after that. I thought he'd stopped riding."

Libby and Amanda looked at each other with wide eyes at the mention of the equestrian team.

Sal hooked his thumbs in his jeans pockets. "Well, guess he's back—and it can't hurt our reputation to have as good a rider as Ian here—even if he didn't make it to the team!"

"I told Ian about High Hopes!" Libby exclaimed, but none of the adults paid any attention to her.

The bay Libby had seen Ian ride at the show poked his head over his door and Emily rubbed his face. "At least it will get us through the next month, anyway."

Mr. McClave slapped Sal on the back. "Glad to see you smile again!"

Sal laughed and then looked in at the gray horse and nodded to himself. "No one can say Sal Ricci's stable is washed up now with this guy around," he muttered.

"Is Ian here?" Libby asked. Sal glanced at her as if he'd just noticed her for the first time.

"Libby, go get Saddleshoes ready. I'll meet you in the ring, there you go."

It was so great to see Sal happy again, even if no one knew that she had been the one to tell Ian about High Hopes in the first place!

So Project Blue Ribbons had worked—just not in the way that Libby had expected. And getting Ian to board here was only the beginning! As Libby made her way to the tack room she noticed there was no sign of Brittany, who always rode on Monday. Now Libby knew Brittany had to be really feeling sorry for herself, but how many times had Libby lost to Brittany? Maybe it was high time someone else beat her at something. Libby couldn't believe that little Amanda had been the one to change things this way.

As soon as Libby got to Saddleshoes's stall the pony immediately put his ears back and turned his hindquarters to her. One thing hadn't changed. She held out a carrot. "Come on, boy," she said quietly. He flicked his ears forward like he had the other day, but by the time she got to the ring he had already shied twice.

Emily worked with Amanda and Libby waited for Sal. And waited . . . and waited . . .

Finally she heard the familiar "Shorten your reins, Libby!"

Sal leaned on the rail of the ring and waved her over. "I'm running late today, so just work on your own. Do

some transitions and stay at the trot and I'll give you a lesson on Wednesday."

"Okay," she said, even though she didn't think it was okay. She had been looking forward to Sal helping her, but he was always busy these days.

Sal turned to go when Libby thought of something. "Is Ian going to ride today?"

"He can only ride in the mornings during the week," Sal said.

"How early?" Libby wanted to know.

Sal pushed himself away from the fence. "'Bout five thirty."

"Sunrise?" Libby said, surprised. She'd never heard of anyone riding that early.

"Yep, sunrise." Sal walked away with his usual uneven gait.

Libby still stood at the rail. "But how will I see him ride?"

He called to her over his shoulder, "Guess you'll have to wait till the weekend."

13

IAN

But Libby had decided that she couldn't wait until the weekend.

She stood in her pajamas that night at the foot of the stairs and shouted into the family room, "I'm going to bed, everybody!" Her mother and father and Laurel turned from the TV in astonishment.

"See you in the morning." Libby staged a yawn and then bolted up the stairs before anyone could ask her why she was suddenly going to bed at 8:00 p.m. Even

Margaret was confused and stood in the middle of Libby's bedroom blinking, unsure of whether it was worth the effort to jump on the bed if they were just going to go back downstairs in two minutes.

Libby set the alarm for five fifteen. "There," she said, and climbed into bed.

She lay in the dark trying to fall asleep but she couldn't stop stewing over everything that had happened to lead up to this moment, beginning with Princess being yanked away from her and ending with everybody going to the show—including Brittany, who hadn't even been riding as long as she had. Added to that, Sal had problems of his own, and she couldn't always rely on him.

Emily had said that Ian was the best rider she'd seen. But how had he gotten so good? Libby remembered how she had learned to ride by watching Laurel, and now she would learn by watching the best—Ian—tomorrow at five thirty.

She slept lightly that night, and even before the first sounds of the birds at dawn she was awake. Margaret snored softly and Libby got out of bed carefully so as not to disturb her. It was 5:10. The alarm hadn't even gone off yet and she pushed the button now to make sure that it didn't. She dressed quickly in the dark and tiptoed out of her room.

"What are you doing?" Laurel called to her sleepily.

"Shhhh," Libby hissed. "Don't tell—I'm going to the barn."

"You're crazy," Laurel muttered, and turned over to go back to sleep.

Downstairs Libby grabbed an apple from the kitchen and a moment later she was outside. It was barely light as she hurried to the park. Fog clung to the ground eerily on the trail that led to High Hopes and now Libby wondered if maybe Laurel had been right: Maybe this idea of hers *was* crazy. What if her mother got up early and found her gone? Libby knew she would be in Big Trouble. She stopped and stood still, unsure of whether or not to turn around. It wasn't too late; she could go back home and no one would ever know, but then she started to think about Amanda and how determined she was to be a top rider and to try out for the equestrian team. She thought about how Sal had laughed with delight to see her jump Cough Drop when no one else could. Libby shook her head and pressed on. Soon she could smell the horses and the hay. She picked up the pace and minutes later she could see the ring next to the barn, bathed in blue mist.

Libby's feet made a crunching sound on the gravel. An unfamiliar beat-up old red Ford truck sat in the driveway.

There he was!

Ian walked around in a tight circle to the right while the bay horse traveled around him at the end of a long white tether that Libby knew was called a "lunge line." In his left hand was an equally long whip, which he kept low just behind the horse's hind quarters to keep him moving forward. Ian had on jeans and half chaps that were shiny on the insides of his legs from wear. All around was quiet except for the horse's rhythmic breathing, the strikes from his hooves trotting in the sand, and the sound the leather saddle made when it stretched and retracted in time to his trot.

"Canter," Ian said. The horse easily picked up the steady three-beat gait. He seemed to understand every command that Ian uttered.

Libby leaned on the rail and watched, spellbound.

"Walk," Ian commanded, and the horse obeyed immediately.

Ian went to him and patted his neck, then took off the lunge line. He was going to ride!

He warmed the bay up the same way that Sal had taught them by doing circles and transitions. Ian seemed to be completely oblivious to her presence. So that when he walked by fifteen minutes later Libby was shocked when he spoke to her.

"You're just in time," he mumbled.

"I am?" Libby said, flustered. "For what?"

"To be my jump crew again." He gestured for her to come into the ring. She climbed through the fence and was soon setting up a rail after the cavaletti. He had her put up the fence a stride after the first jump to make it an

in-and-out. He had her raise some of the other jumps in the ring and Libby had to run over to replace a rail that his horse had knocked down.

When Ian was done he thanked her. "You must be my jump-crew fairy," he teased. "You appear out of nowhere." He relaxed into a slouch and walked his horse on a long rein around Libby. Then halted and jumped off the horse. He put up his stirrups.

Libby marveled that his horse stood perfectly still. He had a white star between his eyes. "He's so beautiful." Libby patted his neck that was still sweaty. "What's his name?"

"Armstrong," Ian said.

"He's perfect," Libby said.

Ian made a face. He loosened the girth and Armstrong reached around with his head and tried to nip. "No!" Ian said firmly, and the horse stood now at attention. "Still haven't broken him of that."

"The pony I ride does the same thing!" Libby exclaimed. "He's really bad."

"You should have seen this guy a few months ago," Ian said.

"Really? He wasn't always like this?" Libby asked.

Ian spoke with his back to Libby as he undid his horse's noseband. "He was *terrible* to ride in the beginning."

Libby was surprised.

"You don't believe me?" Ian said, bemused. He took off his helmet and had curly black hair that was starting to recede even though he was still young.

"It's not that I don't believe you—it's just that my pony, Saddleshoes, is terrible to ride too—and I can't imagine him ever being as good as Armstrong."

"Can I tell you a little secret?" Ian muttered, and Libby had to strain her ears to hear, he talked so softly. "Some of the best horses were the worst to ride in the beginning."

"Really?" Libby had never heard of this—but then there were a lot of things she'd never heard of. She scrunched up her nose. "How old are you?"

"Twenty-two. Sounds really old, doesn't it?" Ian teased.

Libby shook her head. "Why do you ride so early?"

"I have to be at work by nine o'clock." Ian started toward the barn with long strides and Libby had to trot to keep up.

"What kind of work?" she asked.

"It's very exciting. . . ." Ian smirked.

"It is?" Libby said excitedly.

"I'm a teller at a bank."

Libby walked alongside Ian and squinted her eyes as she looked at his profile. She shook her head. "You don't look at all like a teller at a bank."

Ian laughed. "What do I look like?"

Libby grinned and answered right away, "A rider." Suddenly Libby got the best idea. "Can I ride with you one morning?"

Ian stopped and turned to Libby. He laughed softly. "Now, why would you want to do that?"

"Because I think . . . I mean I hope . . . I mean I *need* to try to find out if I have the potential to be a really good rider someday—just like you."

Ian shook his head. "You don't want to be like me."

"Yes I do! Emily said that you were picked to train on the equestrian team!" Libby bit her lip because she knew she probably shouldn't ask, but she couldn't help herself. "Why didn't you go?"

Ian turned away and walked quickly. They had reached the barn. "I blew it," he said curtly, and walked through the doorway.

Libby was sorry she'd asked. She hoped she hadn't ruined everything. "Ian!" she called. "So . . . can I ride with you?"

He stopped and turned again. Libby could see his face still looked tense and unhappy but his expression suddenly softened. He raised his chin. "Sure."

"Wow! Thanks!" Libby called back to him. She started to run off; it was getting late and she had to get home, but then she remembered something and ran back.

"Ian!" she yelled through the barn door. "Can my friend Amanda come and ride with you too?"

14

PLEASE SAY YES!

"Yes!" Ian said, and disappeared with his horse into a stall.

Libby twirled around and her feet barely touched the ground as she ran all the way home. She couldn't wait to tell Amanda!

Now all she had to do was get inside the house and change her shoes that were wet from the grass without being caught. Her watch said 6:24. It was still early.

She tried to calm herself down as she went through the garage to the laundry room so that she could get upstairs without having to go through the kitchen.

She was only halfway up the stairs when she heard, "*Libbyyyyyy!*"

Busted! Libby thought. "Coming!" she yelled, and flew back down the stairs. She skidded into the kitchen and her mother looked up from where she stood by the toaster.

"Well, look at you, all bright-eyed and bushy-tailed so early!" She smiled. "I've been calling you—where've you been?"

Libby had to think fast. "I went out for a walk—it was such a beautiful morning!" She busied herself with Margaret's breakfast and tried to appear as normal as possible.

"Good for you, honey!" The toast popped up. Mrs. Thump put one piece on a plate for Libby. She spoke in a low voice now. "Oh, how I wish Laurel was more like you." She glanced at Libby as she buttered the toast. "You make me feel so guilty, Libby—I should've been out running by now!"

Libby made a lame little laugh—if anyone should feel guilty it was her! She filled the dog's bowl with kibble and gave it to Margaret. Then she went to the refrigerator to get some juice.

"Anyway, Libby, I need to talk to you about Brittany," Mrs. Thump said.

Libby looked up, surprised. "Brittany?"

"Have you seen her lately?" her mother asked.

"Um—I saw her in school yesterday but I didn't get a chance to talk to her." *Because she wasn't speaking to me*, Libby thought.

Mrs. Thump continued, "Her mother says she's *very* upset about the show."

Libby knew that was the understatement of the year. "Yeah, she got eliminated in the class that Amanda got first place in."

"Her mother says she's really down about it—could

you talk to her, sweetie?" Mrs. Thump handed Libby her toast. "You two have been friends for so long— I'm sure you can make her feel better."

Libby considered this as she ate, and now she really did feel a little badly for Brittany even though Brittany was still mad at her. She hadn't even thought of asking Ian if Brittany could ride with them in the mornings too, but Brittany wasn't really serious about horses— not like Amanda, anyway. Still, it was hard to see her lose and be so unhappy about it. Brittany was not supposed to lose. It was practically a law of nature. "Don't worry, Mom. I'll talk to her."

But Libby had other things on her mind and by now she was on fire to ask her mother if she could ride with Ian . . . she just didn't know how. "Mom? I've been thinking." Libby frowned, trying to figure out how to say it. "There's this really good rider at the barn, named Ian?"

Mrs. Thump raised her eyebrows expectantly. "Ian?"

Libby pressed on. "Okay, so he rides like around five thirty in the morning—that's sunrise?"

"I've heard of sunrise, Libby." Her mother laughed.

"Okay, great," Libby continued. "But here's the thing . . . it would be really good for my riding to ride with him say, two times a week." Libby hesitated at this part because she knew she was going to be met with resistance. "Like before school?" Libby spoke quickly now. "I could learn so much—just by watching him. Please say yes!"

Mrs. Thump put down her coffee cup. "I think that's an excellent idea, Libby!"

"You do?" Libby said in disbelief.

"Yes, I do."

At this point Laurel shuffled in sleepily, still in her pajamas, and sat down at the table.

"In fact"—Mrs. Thump eyed her older daughter—"I think we should *all* get up earlier."

It got very quiet until Laurel realized her mother

was referring to her and finally said a little defensively, "What?"

"Libby is going to ride before school two days a week and I think we should all get up early with her! I'm going to do my runs on those days. Want to come?"

"Not really," Laurel muttered. She raked her fingers through her long blond hair and into a ponytail, then twisted it all around only to let it all go. It was a mannerism her sister constantly performed, the purpose of which Libby still hadn't figured out.

"Well I think it sounds like fun, we'll get a nice head start on summer!" Her mother spoke louder over the noise of running water as she rinsed out her coffee cup. "We could even think about doing that 5K race at the end of June."

"What are we doing?" Libby's father entered the kitchen.

"We're all going to get up early now that it's almost summer."

"But why?" he asked.

"Because we're missing the best part of the day!" Mrs. Thump opened the sliding glass doors and walked out to the porch. "Just smell that air! We should all try to be more like Libby!"

"I know *I'm* going to try to be more like Libby," her father said, and he went to make his coffee.

Laurel rolled her eyes.

Libby was astonished. She was really going to ride with Ian—she couldn't wait to tell Amanda!

All morning in class, no matter what Libby did, she couldn't get Brittany's attention. She was determined to talk to her, so as soon as the bell rang at lunchtime Libby sprang out of her seat but Brittany was too fast.

"Hey, Brit! Wait up!" Libby ran after her.

They walked down the hall toward the cafeteria and Libby could immediately tell that this wasn't going to be so easy. "I'm really sorry that you had a bad day at the show."

Brittany stared straight ahead. Her lime-green ballet flats made a sharp *tap! tap! tap!* sound on the tile floor. "I thought you were going to come for moral support, Libby," Brittany said coldly.

"I did come," Libby protested.

"Yeah, after everything was over," Brittany said in a hurt voice.

Libby tried to explain to her friend. "I'm really sorry, Brit, I did start out by looking for you when I first got to the show but then I ran into Emily and had to help her and then someone else asked me to set up fences. Before I knew it you were in the ring."

"Yeah, what a disaster," Brittany said glumly.

"You couldn't help it—Summer acted the same way with Laurel, remember?" Libby continued on in a more excited tone. "But look, what I wanted to tell you is that there's another horse show on the twenty-first, so you'll have another chance—"

"I'm sure *Amanda* is riding," Brittany said, and sneered.

"Probably, I mean yeah," Libby answered.

Brittany turned to Libby now for the first time. "I don't know why you think she's so great."

Libby opened her eyes wide and looked at the floor as she walked. "I don't think Amanda is 'so great.' I think she's a good rider—and I kind of feel a little sorry for her—she doesn't seem to have any friends."

"Yeah, I wonder why," Brittany said under her breath.

"What do you mean?" Libby asked, because she really didn't know why Brittany didn't like her.

"I don't trust her," Brittany said. Her light brown perfect hair bounced on top of her shoulders.

Libby couldn't have been more surprised. "Why don't you trust her?"

"Wake up, Libby!" Brittany exclaimed. "I think she'd take Saddleshoes from you in a minute if she could—but you don't see it."

Libby *didn't* see it. "Why do you say that?"

Brittany halted just outside the cafeteria and kids swarmed around them on either side. She lowered her voice. "My mom and her mom sell real estate from the same office—and my mom said that Amanda's mother came in yesterday showing video and pictures and bragging about the blue ribbon Amanda won at the show—and then asked my mother how *I* did, when she knew very well I did terrible!" Brittany shook her head.

"But Brit, the way her mom acts isn't Amanda's fault," Libby reasoned.

"That's not all," Brittany said. She pulled Libby by the sleeve off to the side into an alcove by the water fountain and whispered, "I didn't want to upset you so I didn't tell you at the time, but the week that you were gone I heard her mother ask Sal if Amanda could ride Saddleshoes at the show."

Libby's mind reeled and she felt a little dizzy for a second until she realized she'd actually momentarily stopped breathing. "But that's *still* not Amanda's fault."

"Amanda stood right next to her mother the entire time her mother talked to Sal. Sal said no—thank goodness." Libby knew Brittany wouldn't lie, but she also knew that Brittany couldn't stand being beat by Amanda—maybe she was exaggerating.

"Are you sure?" Libby thought there had to be some other explanation.

Brittany stood with her hands on her hips. "You think I'd make that up?" she said indignantly.

Libby didn't know what to think. "No, but maybe you heard it wrong. . . . Maybe there's something you missed—I don't know—I can't imagine that Amanda would—"

Brittany tossed her head. "All right—forget I said anything." She turned and walked into the cafeteria.

Libby followed in disbelief and tried to change the subject. "Come to the barn this week, Brittany—please say yes?"

Just then Libby saw Amanda wave from her a table off in the corner. Libby waved back. "So you'll come?" she asked, anxious to end her conversation with Brittany so that she could get over to Amanda and tell her the news.

"Maybe," Brittany said unconvincingly.

Libby quickly excused herself from Brittany and made a beeline over to the other girl's table. "Wait till you hear!"

Amanda was sitting alone as usual. She looked happy to see Libby and pulled out a seat. Libby sat and the words tumbled out of her mouth excitedly. They were really going to get to ride with someone who had almost ridden on the equestrian team! As she delivered the news about Ian everything that Brittany had just told her faded, and Libby forgot all about it.

15

SUNRISE

Everybody set your alarms!" Mrs. Thump announced on Sunday night. Libby's arm didn't hurt at all anymore and she had been excitedly waiting all week for the agreed-upon day of Monday when she and Amanda could start their rides with Ian. "We're getting up at five fifteen, people!" It was only eight thirty but the entire family was in their pajamas.

Amanda had even been allowed to spend the night to keep her mother from having to drive her to the barn so early. Libby had her whole outfit laid out to save time in the morning. She placed everything on her drawing table and stood trying to decide about what top to wear. It was the first day of June but would still be cool that early in the morning. "Are you wearing a long-sleeve shirt tomorrow?" Libby asked, but Amanda was already fast asleep, which was weird because when Brit or Mim slept over they always talked until Laurel stomped in to yell at them. Amanda was different in lots of ways, and this was just another.

That night it felt to Libby that she'd hardly closed her eyes when the alarm went off. The girls hurried to get dressed for their first ride with Ian. Libby gave her boots a few more swipes with the brush to shine them up. She wanted to look her best this morning. She glanced at the closed door to the bathroom and stifled a smile. Amanda was one of those kids who turned around to change her shirt. She'd gone into the bathroom with her entire outfit—including her boots. But when she emerged Libby's jaw dropped. "You're wearing *breeches*?" Libby was wearing just her old jeans and boots. She was saving her breeches for the horse show.

"Why didn't you tell me?" Libby said, disappointed. Amanda even had a piece of thick bright pink yarn tied to each one of her pigtails.

Amanda held a hand to her mouth. "Oh! I'm sorry! I didn't even think to tell you—but you look fine."

Libby thought that Amanda looked just like a mini version of a real equestrian team rider. It was too late for her to pull off her boots, change into her fancy riding pants, and find yarn for her braids. It would have to wait till their next ride.

The girls bolted their breakfasts and passed Mrs. Thump and a half-asleep Laurel all dressed for her first run while Mr. Thump had Margaret on her leash ready for an early morning walk. All the Thumps were out the door by five thirty.

Libby and Amanda ran through the misty twilit morning; it was so quiet it felt as though they were the only people in the world. In the woods it was still except for a deer they spotted and some rabbits that skittered across their path. But even the beautiful morning couldn't distract Libby from her worries about the brown-and-white pony. What would he be like today? She called up ahead to Amanda, who walked briskly. "Ian says that some of the worst horses turn out to be the best jumpers." Amanda didn't answer, She was too far away to hear.

At the barn the sun was still low and the trees cast the ring into shadow. Sal had dragged the ring the night before but the sand was already chewed up from Ian's first ride.

"Riding with the pied piper, I see," Sal said as soon as he saw Libby that morning. He'd come to call Ian that. The young man had stoically tolerated the girls who had followed him around like two puppy dogs all weekend, asking questions.

By the time Libby and Amanda joined him he was on his second horse, the big gray. His lanky frame hunched a little as he walked his horse and Libby couldn't help to think of the character in the Sleepy Hollow tale, Ichabod Crane. Ian had the same long, thin arms and legs and bony knees and elbows that she'd seen in pictures. "Well, well, well. If it isn't the jump-crew fairy and her fine feathered friend!"

Amanda soon was trotting Cough Drop, the pink yarn fluttering prettily from her pigtails, and Libby thought she looked more and more like she was ready for the Olympics. But Saddleshoes threw his head, shied, and jigged. Who was she kidding? She was never going to be able to ride this pony. It was hopeless.

Ian finished schooling the gray horse and Libby had hardly even had a chance to watch; she had her hands full just staying on the spotted pony. He walked his horse to cool him off and joked with Amanda. "I don't believe that fat pony can jump!"

"Oh, yes, he can!" Amanda said with delight, as if it were a dare.

"I'll bet he can't even get over that pole on the ground," he kidded.

"I'll bet he can!" Amanda gathered her reins and took off like a shot. Cough Drop seemed transformed into a completely brand-new pony as she made him jump around a course of fences. She finally pulled up and Ian clapped his hands.

Meanwhile Libby struggled. Ian walked his horse around and around the ring, cooling him off, and Libby knew he was watching her. She could feel her face grow red and hot with embarrassment. She hadn't even tried to canter. All she'd done so far was walk and try to trot. It was humiliating.

Ian left the ring without a word. Libby rode up beside Amanda. Saddleshoes jigged and flipped his head. "Ian will probably never let me ride with you guys ever again," Libby mumbled. "I wouldn't blame him." Amanda raised her eyebrows but didn't say anything reassuring. Libby was about to take the pony back to the barn in disgrace, when Ian entered the ring. He had put his horse away and was back!

"Hey, Libby!" Ian was calling to her.

They all stood now in the center of the ring. "How about if I get on that pony a second?"

"You want to?" Libby said shyly.

"If you don't mind—I want to see something."

Saddleshoes eyed Ian warily as he approached.

"He doesn't stand when you get on him," Libby warned.

Right away Saddleshoes began to back up and dance around. Ian took him over to the rail of the ring so that he couldn't go sideways. He took hold of the bridle by the bit. "Stand," he said firmly. After several tries Saddleshoes gave up and stood.

Ian looked funny and way too big on the pony. Libby watched him walk, trot, and canter. Saddleshoes picked up the wrong lead at first, just like he always did with her, but then Ian got him on the correct lead. "Yay!" Libby shouted.

After about ten minutes Ian handed the pony back to Libby and said, "He's very timid."

"Saddleshoes?" Libby said incredulously. "Timid—like, afraid? Of what?"

"Everything. He needs a confident rider, Libby. You have to take the lead here."

"I do?" she said, not quite sure of what he meant.

"He's waiting for you to tell him what to do." Ian gave Saddleshoes some loud pats on his neck. "He's a really nice pony! And I'll bet he's a good jumper, too!"

Amanda was listening and said, "I jumped him in a kimberwick and he was much easier to control."

"Yes," Ian replied. "That's a good idea—but just for jumping. He needs to learn how to go in a snaffle on the flat."

Ian gave Libby a leg up and the pony never moved. "Now you try," he said.

She could immediately feel the difference.

"Shorten your reins and keep your leg on him, Libby. Lots of circles and transitions to keep him occupied!"

For the first time Libby felt encouraged. She couldn't

believe how much Ian had helped her already, and at school that day she couldn't stop thinking about it. It wasn't going to be easy and there wasn't a lot of time, but if she could just pay attention and do everything Ian told her, Libby knew she could get to the show and win her class.

She glanced at the clock on the wall in Mr. Kaufman's class for the hundredth time. What had Amanda thought of her ride that morning? Libby was anxious to get to lunch to talk it all over with her.

The bell finally rang and Libby hurried out into the hall. Up ahead were Mim and Brittany. Brittany had gotten over her hurt feelings and was back sitting at their usual table eating lunch just like the three of them had since first grade, but in the cafeteria Libby went in the opposite direction. She knew her old friends would think it was weird that she wasn't having lunch with them, but Libby just *had* to talk to Amanda—now.

"Isn't Ian awesome?" Libby said excitedly as she pulled up a chair to sit with Amanda.

"He's awesome!" Amanda agreed. "I can't wait for Friday!"

Libby glanced over at Mim and Brittany and they immediately looked away. They definitely thought she was being weird but Libby also knew she had her work cut out for her. She couldn't wait for Friday either! Ian had told her to do lots of transitions and circles with Saddleshoes. She would have to practice this the next day, and then there was her lesson with Sal on Wednesday, and Libby soon forgot about her other two friends.

On Wednesday Sal shouted, "Very good!" to her when the pony finally took the correct lead. "I see a lot of improvement," he said happily.

"Really?" Libby asked eagerly. "Do you think I'll be able to ride him in the show, Sal?"

"If you keep improving, I don't see why not!" Sal turned to leave the ring.

Brittany rode at the other end of the ring and called out, "Saddleshoes looks good, Libby!"

"Thanks!" Libby called back, and braced herself. Sal was gone and now Brittany was riding over to her. She wanted to talk. Just as Libby thought, as soon as she told Brittany that there was another show, she'd shown up at the barn the next day. Libby knew her old best friend could never pass up a chance to redeem herself and try to beat Amanda.

"He's going so well for you," Brittany said in her nicest voice. They walked side by side around the ring. Brittany glanced at Libby and sounded almost shy. "Libby? I'm—I'm sorry I had to tell you about Amanda. I hope—"

"It's okay, Brit—really, it's all right," Libby interrupted. She didn't want to hurt Brittany's feelings but Libby didn't want to hear anything more that Brittany had to say about her friend Amanda. She rode away and left the ring.

16

GREAT EXPECTATIONS

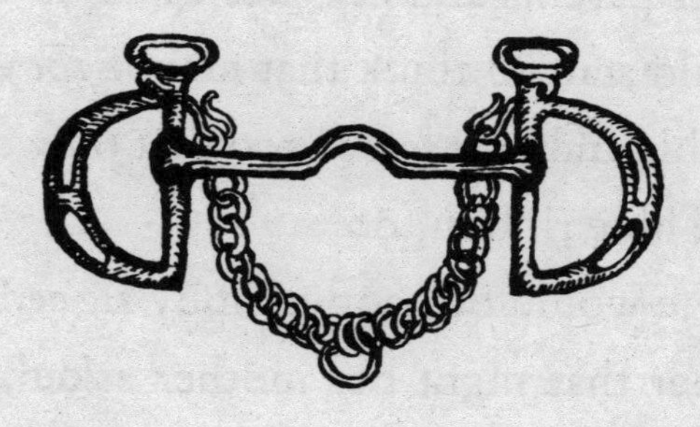

PROJECT BLUE RIBBONS!!!
We are improving!
Goal #1: Jump Saddleshoes in the horse show!
Goal #2: Win a blue ribbon!

Next Libby made a sign and taped it to her mirror that said:

June 21st: Win blue ribbon!

Libby tried to imagine what it would be like to really win a blue ribbon. Sal would be so proud! She could see the judge pinning it on Saddleshoes's bridle right in front of her parents and her sister. People would clap. Some would start to think that maybe *they* should go to Sal's stable and take lessons so that they could win a satin royal blue ribbon too.

Everyone would be happy. Libby sighed.

At dinner that night her mother asked, "How's it going with Saddleshoes?"

"Great!" Libby exclaimed. Writing it all down in her Project Blue Ribbons notebook had made her feel like it'd kind of already happened. "There's a show on June twenty-first, and Sal said if I keep improving I'll be able to ride Saddleshoes in it—I might even win a blue ribbon!"

Laurel's mouth dropped open. "That's amazing!" Libby knew her sister was genuinely impressed. "What classes will you be in?" Laurel asked.

"Probably walk, trot, canter, and a jumping class for

JUNE 21ST
WIN BLUE
RIBBON!

sure," Libby said confidently, even though she hadn't jumped the pony yet.

Laurel shook her head. "Wow! Good for you, Lib!"

"We'll all come and cheer you on," her mother said.

"I know you'll do great!" her father said proudly.

Libby suddenly had a fluttery feeling in her stomach. What if Saddleshoes didn't continue to improve . . . if Sal didn't even let her go to the show? It was one thing for *her* to think she would do great—she was always thinking crazy stuff that never happened—but it was another thing altogether for everyone in her family to expect it. . . . It was a lot to live up to. She changed the subject.

"How was your run on Monday?" Libby asked.

Her mother glanced at Laurel slyly. "Believe it or not, she left me in the dust."

"Really?" Libby had no idea that Laurel was a good runner. All her sister ever did was walk around with her eyes glued to her phone.

"I think we have a blossoming track star on our hands." Mr. Thump winked.

Laurel made light of it and only said, "Beginner's luck."

"I'm going to enter that 5K on the twenty-second," Mrs. Thump said. "What do you think, Laurel?"

"Okay." Laurel remained nonchalant.

Libby was even more surprised now.

So was her mother. "Really?" she said hopefully.

"Sure," Laurel answered.

Mrs. Thump took a second helping of rice. "I'd better start carb-loading now."

Everyone laughed, and then there was lull in the conversation.

Libby's mother turned to her. "Honey, I've been meaning to ask—did you ever speak with Brittany? You know, about the show?"

Did I ever, Libby thought, and remembered how Brittany had given her an earful about Amanda. "Um, yeah," Libby said, and became aware of her heart that was thudding inside her chest.

"Did you make her feel better—about her bad day at the show?" her mother asked.

Libby pushed a strand of hair behind her ear. "Oh, yes—she's fine. She's excited about this next show coming up."

"Well, that's good." Mrs. Thump continued, "I know you're having fun riding with Amanda and Ian, but you shouldn't forget about your old friends, okay, honey?"

Libby shifted uncomfortably in her seat. "Oh, I won't," she replied.

"Good!" her mother said, satisfied.

But her mother's warning was easier said than done because at school the next day, Libby steered clear of Brittany and Brittany seemed to do the same. The last bell finally rang and Libby swung her backpack onto her shoulder, eager to get home. She had homework to do and then had to get to bed to be ready for another early morning ride with Amanda and Ian.

"Libby, wait!" Mim trotted up next to her as she walked to the bus.

"Do you want to go to the movies tomorrow night?

My mom said she'd take me and you and Brit to dinner too!"

Libby loved going to the movies with Mim and Brittany. They always ate too much popcorn and made way too much noise giggling, and Mim's mother always fake-scolded them and said she was going to call the movie-theater police if they didn't simmer down. But Libby knew she had to get up at five o'clock on Friday to ride, go to school all day, and get home to do her homework. She'd planned to spend the entire weekend at the barn with Amanda so that they could hang around and watch Ian ride his horses. Libby shook her head. "I can't, Mim—sorry."

Mim pulled her upper lip down and looked disappointed. "Libby," she said hesitantly, "is everything all right between you and Brittany?"

"Yes," Libby said nervously.

Mim frowned. "It's just that . . . Brittany said she thought you were mad at her."

"I'm not, Mim," Libby said. "I'm working really

hard to get Saddleshoes ready for the show and I need to ride every day."

"Okay," Mim said in a small voice.

"Okay," Libby replied, but she could tell Mim didn't understand. Libby knew that Brittany wouldn't understand either that sometimes to be a really good rider you had to say no to your friends when you got invited to the movies. That sometimes that's what it takes to be a really good rider. Libby couldn't wait to tell Amanda.

"That's what it takes," Amanda agreed sternly the next morning on their way out to the ring to ride with Ian.

Libby made herself forget about Mim and Brittany going to the movies without her that night and concentrated on Saddleshoes to make him go as well as he had all week. She wanted to look good today and had tied pink yarn on the end of her braids and even worn her breeches just like Amanda.

"Where's our jump-crew fairy?" Ian asked, turning

all the way around in the saddle soon after Libby entered the ring.

"Here." Libby waved a hand halfheartedly. She didn't want to be anybody's jump crew. She wanted to jump just like Amanda. But how could she say no to Ian? He'd been so nice in letting her and Amanda ride with him.

Libby got off Saddleshoes and led him around as she placed the striped poles in their cups.

"A little higher, please?" Ian called to her, and she pulled the pin out of the metal cup and slid it to up to the next hole in the jump's standard. Amanda headed Cough Drop toward a brush box with a red-and-white pole over it. The pony had never looked so good. He had lost a lot of fat from the increased work and Amanda had pulled his mane and cut off his long, bushy tail. All the shaggy hair from winter had been curried away to reveal a sleek, dappled summer coat. He looked like a completely different pony.

"Awesome!" Ian shouted as Cough Drop sailed

over another fence. And now the old feelings of discouragement began to creep back into Libby's mind.

"Let's see what that spotted pony can do," Ian said, and he turned his attention to her, but this made Libby feel even worse when she had to say, "I've never jumped him."

"Never mind," Ian hopped off his horse. He picked something up off the top of the fence post. "Look what I brought." From the young man's fingers dangled a bit.

Libby was once again on the sidelines. She held Ian's horse this time as he headed the pony through the cavaletti. He trotted him over a small crossbar and Saddleshoes tried to run out, but Ian kept him from doing that and got him over the jump. They trotted over several more small fences, but now Libby couldn't believe her eyes because the more he jumped the pony, the better Saddleshoes got. Ian cantered him over a gate and Saddleshoes tucked his front legs just like Ian's horse had. He didn't even rush the fences like he had with Kate. Finally

Ian walked, dropped the reins, and patted the pony loudly on the neck.

"You've got a great pony here, Libby, and you don't even know it!"

"I do?"

Ian nodded. "He's not the easiest to ride, for sure, but he can sure jump!"

"Really?" Libby said.

Ian swung his leg over the front of the saddle and hopped off. He handed her the reins. "Really. And you can keep the bit!"

"Wow! Thanks, Ian!" Libby ran a finger around the metal D rings. It was shiny and sparkled in the sun, and she vowed to always keep it that way.

That night she wrote in her Project Blue Ribbons notebook:

Ian jumped Saddleshoes today.
He thinks he's a good jumper.

I'm going to jump him on Monday!!! Ian gave me a bit to keep!!!!

Over the weekend Libby worked on trotting Saddleshoes through the cavaletti. She tried to remember everything Ian had said: to keep her legs on him, to be clear and firm, to take the lead. She closed her eyes and pictured in her mind how Ian had looked riding the pony and tried to look just like him. She also tried to avoid Brittany when she came to the barn to ride on Sunday, but late in the afternoon on her way home there was no avoiding the other girl because there was Brittany, leaning over the fence and feeding Princess a carrot.

"Hey," Libby mumbled on her way through the paddock.

"Hey," Brittany said back.

"How was the movie?" Libby said as she passed.

"Really fun," Brittany said. "I wish you could have come."

"Me too," Libby muttered.

As Libby made her way up the hill she felt sad. She felt like she should have stopped to talk to Brittany. That she should have stopped to see Princess and feed her a carrot as well. She felt like she wished she'd gone to the movies on Friday night with her friends and that things were the way they used to be, but she also knew that really good riders had to make sacrifices. Amanda was right when she told Libby, "my mother says that it takes a long time to get good—all I need to do is just think about my riding." As Libby made her way back home, she strengthened her resolve to do the best she could on Saddleshoes.

It was hard to wake up on Monday morning. Libby was more tired than usual but she made herself get out of bed. When she walked into the barn at 6:00 a.m. she was still thinking about Mim and Brittany and how she'd missed out on going to the movies, when suddenly she heard a sound. Libby looked up to see Saddleshoes's head hanging over the stall door, and now the sound was louder.

"He's been waiting for you," Emily laughed.

Libby ran to the brown-and-white pony and put her arms around his neck. For the first time he had nickered to her just the way Princess always did. Libby fed him a carrot. "Good boy," she whispered. It was just the lift Libby needed. This was proof! All her hard work really *was* making a difference.

She took her time grooming him, taking care not to scare him when she worked around his head. When he moved she took hold of his halter and said, "Stand," in a firm tone of voice just the way Ian had. She leaned against his shoulder to pick up each foot and clean it out. The she painted his hooves like Amanda always did to Cough Drop.

Before she headed out to the ring, she stroked Saddleshoes's neck. "Okay, boy. We're going to a show in two weeks—but you've got to do well today;

this is important." Saddleshoes looked at her with serious eyes.

Out in the ring Ian and Amanda rode around talking and laughing, but Libby was all business today. She was going to jump!

"Now you try," Ian said after he had jumped his horse and Amanda had done a course with Cough Drop. They both came to the middle of the ring to watch.

Libby took a deep breath and whispered as she changed his bit, "Remember, Shoes, you're going to do really well today."

Before she had a chance to think about it too much more she was trotting through the poles like she had all weekend. Ian put up a crossbar after the cavaletti and Saddleshoes jumped it just like she had with Princess so many weeks ago.

"Now trot the small fences like I did," Ian called to her. Saddleshoes immediately tried to break into a canter, but with the new bit she was able to bring him back down to a trot and keep him there. "Keep your leg on him and get him in straight!" Ian instructed. Ian walked to the corner of the ring and put up a rail straight across where a small crossbar had been. "Now pick up a canter and come over this fence." It was higher and Libby wasn't sure.

"Ride him like you mean it, Libby!" Ian shouted.

She took a shorter hold and closed her legs on the pony's sides. One . . . two . . . three strides . . . Jump! She was over.

"Yeah!" Ian grinned. "I told you!"

"Good boy!" Libby patted his neck loudly just like Ian had the other day.

Amanda left the ring right away but Libby lingered, basking in the joy of having jumped Saddleshoes for the first time. Maybe she really would get to that horse show! "Thanks for all your help, Ian."

Ian got off his horse and loosened the girth. "You're trying really hard, Libby, and it's starting to pay off." He looked at his watch and Libby knew he needed to hurry. If only he didn't have to be a bank teller . . . he could help a lot of other kids like he had her. "Ian!" Libby exclaimed. "I just figured out a way for you to not have to be a bank teller anymore!"

A smile tugged at his lips as he led his horse out of the ring.

"Wait! Wait!" Libby followed after him. "You should teach riding! You're really good at it and I'll bet you'd make a lot of money!"

Ian mumbled, "You'd be surprised at the opportunities there are these days for people in the bank-teller business."

"But you're a fantastic rider, Ian." Libby didn't understand why he couldn't see that this was the answer to all his problems! "You have to live up to your potential!"

Ian shook his head. "I don't know, sounds pretty hard to do."

"But it's *not*!" Libby said, completely sure of herself

because she had thought about it a lot. "All you have to do is quit your job, start to teach, and try out for the equestrian team again."

Ian stopped at the barn door. "Do you think I have . . . potential, Libby?"

"Oh, tons!" Libby exclaimed. "You *have* to try—my mom says that's the most important thing, is to try—I mean, even if it doesn't work out, at least you know you've tried, right?"

"Is that what you're doing?" Ian asked.

"It's exactly what I'm doing." Libby grinned.

17

MONSTERS AND GOBLINS AND TROLLS!

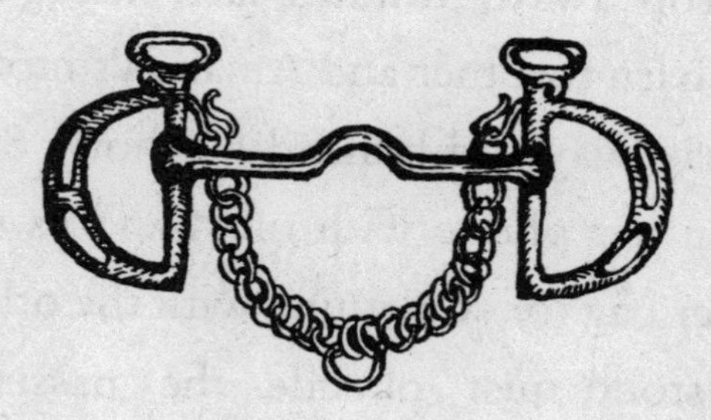

Libby led Saddleshoes into the barn, excited about her morning ride. This was the best that the pony had done by far. She hurried down the aisle to clean him up and get him put away so that she could change and get to school.

Amanda unclipped Cough Drop from the cross ties and pushed him to the side so that Libby could pass. "So I guess you'll be going to the show now?" she asked.

"I don't know—it's up to Sal." Libby paused. "Do you think I will?"

Amanda didn't answer; she was already leading Cough Drop away. Minutes later the girls walked out of the barn together and Amanda's mother pulled into the driveway and honked her horn. She typed a message on her phone with one hand as she clawed through her bag for something with the other.

Libby stood just outside the passenger door as Amanda slid into the car seat. "Libby jumped Saddleshoes today," she said right away.

Instantly her mother looked up from her phone. "You won't be going to the show, though, dear." She shook her head and made a face, as if the idea of Libby going to a show was completely crazy.

"I might," Libby replied now a little unsure.

Amanda's mother gazed at her and shrugged, "Okey, dokey."

As they drove away Libby wondered uneasily what Amanda's mother meant.

• • •

That night Libby wrote in her Project Blue Ribbons notebook: Monday:

I DID IT!!!! I jumped Saddleshoes!!!!

She had accomplished a huge goal. Friday was the last day of school, too. Her most wonderful summer ever was about to begin! So why did Libby have an uneasy feeling? Instead of falling asleep she lay there stewing. What had Amanda's mother meant this afternoon when she'd made a face at the idea of Libby riding Saddleshoes in the show? Had Amanda told her mother that Libby wasn't ready to show the difficult brown-and-white pony? Worse . . . was she right? Libby was filled with doubts now. She wished she could talk to Brittany or Mim about it—they both would have known exactly the right thing to say to make her feel better, but she couldn't very well talk about Amanda or her mother to either one of them.

Plus she and Brittany and Mim weren't exactly talking that much about anything at the moment.

She turned over to try to get more comfortable. Margaret made muffled woofing sounds and her legs twitched like she was chasing a rabbit in her dreams. Libby frowned in the dark. She still didn't even know if Sal would let her show. She would have to make sure Saddleshoes jumped really well at her next lesson.

By the time Sal limped into the ring on Wednesday, Libby was a bundle of nerves. It didn't help that Brittany was there either. Their mothers had paid for their daughters to share a lesson together with Sal. Brittany was unusually subdued. "Shorten your reins, girls," he called out, oblivious to the tension between his two students. Libby was relieved when Sal finally started to warm them up over the cavalettis.

She knew the real test of whether or not she would be allowed to show would come when she had to canter the fences. Brittany and Summer went first and did very well—they would definitely be going to the show over the weekend.

It was Libby's turn next. "Keep your hands low," Sal warned. "If he starts to rush his fences, bring him back to a trot." Libby nodded. She circled at the canter, making sure to keep him in a steady cadence to the first fence, the brush box. "Wait . . . wait," Libby said. They met it perfectly and headed to the next jump, the barrels. They cleared that and jumped the rails, the coop, and the in-and-out.

Sal was impressed. "Saddleshoes is doing really well, Libby!"

Libby joined Brittany and Sal in the center of the ring. "The new bit helps a lot," she said.

"Yes, the kimberwick," Sal agreed.

Brittany leaned over Summer's neck to get a better look but remained quiet.

"He gets strong when you start to jump," Sal said, and nodded. "I can see it's made a big difference."

Libby had to ask, "So . . . can I ride Saddleshoes in the show next weekend?"

Sal smiled broadly. "I don't see why not."

"Can I jump?" Libby asked excitedly.

"I think you're ready!" Sal replied.

Libby grinned. It was just what she had hoped for.

"Both you girls can ride in the under-twelve equitation over fences," Sal said.

Libby glanced at Brittany but she was already off her horse and putting up her stirrups. "Thanks, Sal," she muttered politely, and excused herself. Libby watched her go with a sense of relief, but she was also a little sorry. It would have been fun to share in their excitement that they would both be showing in the same class.

Libby walked back to the barn with Sal.

"Saddleshoes seems a lot happier theses days." Sal patted the pony's neck.

Libby had wanted to ask Sal something and now seemed like the right time. "Ian says that the reason Saddleshoes flattens his ears, and shies, and runs away with kids is because he's afraid. Do you think he's right?"

"Ian is right," Sal said. "I found old Saddleshoes around here on a farm with a bunch of other animals that had been neglected. People in the area adopted the donkeys, horses, and ponies that had been there, and I went to help out as well. This brown-and-white caught my eye but he was in very poor shape. He was thin, and had worms, and his tail was loaded with ticks. I adopted him but as you know, he has lingering problems."

"Poor Saddleshoes!" Libby cried. She got off and patted his neck. "Poor boy," she said again, and turned to Sal. "Why didn't you tell me?"

"I guess it's something I sort of try to forget." Sal shoved his hands into the back pockets of his jeans. "Plus it was a long time ago. Saddleshoes was with me for five or six years before Kate bought him."

Kate! Libby hadn't thought about Kate in a while. For so long she had wanted her to come back and take Saddleshoes, but not now. "Sal, when is Kate coming back?"

"Not for a while Libby," Sal said, and winked. "Don't worry!"

Libby was glad and saw the spotted pony in a completely new light. After she untacked him and wiped off his back, she put him in his stall. He went right to the rear of it but turned his head with his ears flicking back and forth, as if he was trying to make up his mind about her. Why hadn't she thought of this before? Libby wondered. Mr. McClave had told her that she needed to listen to her horse, but all she had done was complain that she'd been given such an awful pony to ride. She pressed her face against the bars and waited until Saddleshoes inched his way over to her. He was so close that she could smell his grassy breath, and when she tried to stroke his nose he let her. He wasn't a bad pony after all—she just hadn't been listening.

Libby thought of Mr. McClave's words on Friday morning when she rode with Ian and Amanda again. "Listen with your eyes to get to know his every move," he had said. Saddleshoes's ears pointed straight ahead, focused like a laser beam on Ian's lunge line, which was coiled over a jump standard like a snake about to strike. A second later the pony dropped his shoulder and wheeled. Two weeks ago Libby would have had a hard time staying on. But this time she was ready for him. She took a firm hold and walked him up to the scary lunge line. "It won't hurt you, boy," she said gently as he stretched out his neck and sniffed it.

Saddleshoes had been talking to her all this time and she had finally heard him. The alert position of his ears told her he thought the noise in the bush wasn't a bird but a monster ready to pounce. The tension on the reins was saying the sound out in the field wasn't a tractor but something big and loud coming for him. If she listened with her eyes, her hands, and her legs, she could tell what he was going to do and stop him before he spooked or tried to run away!

Libby finished her early morning ride and hurried to her last day of school. She couldn't wait for summer to start. She and Amanda would ride with Ian every day. There would be lots of horse shows to go to. The word would get out about Sal's and about the two girls, Amanda and Libby, who were winning at all the shows. People would come back to High Hopes Horse Farm. It was going to be a great summer!

Libby counted the minutes until the end of the day. The final bell rang and she sprang out of her seat. Just before she reached the door, Mim came up beside her.

She smiled broadly, as happy as Libby to have an entire summer to look forward to. "See you at the beach, Libby!" she sang out.

Libby wasn't sure about that. With any luck she would be at the barn all day, every day. "Y-yes—but I probably won't be at the beach as much this summer."

Mim's face fell. "Okay . . . well, see you around," she said, and hurried off.

"See you," Libby called after her, and now she really felt badly—but it was the truth. *I'd much rather be at the barn than the beach*, she thought and almost ran right in Mr. Kaufman.

"Miss Thump!" he said firmly, "Pay attention!" Kids raced past them, eager to get out of school and on with their summers.

"I've been trying—I-I really have been, Mr. Kaufman." Libby stammered. Her fourth grade teacher, Mrs. Williams had been a taskmaster, but this year Mr. Kaufman had been even harder. Libby held her breath and waited to hear what he would say next.

"I know you've been trying," he said a little more softly, "And I've enjoyed having you in my class this year. You only see the best in others, don't you?"

Libby was happily surprised. "I guess so, thanks, Mr. Kaufman."

"Have a great summer, Libby," he smiled and the corners of his eyes crinkled. "But pay attention!" he shook his finger at her.

"I will!" Libby smiled back. "I promise!"

Libby got on the bus greatly relieved but when she

automatically took a seat at the front to avoid Brittany, she felt a pang of regret. The bus rolled to a stop and Brittany passed to get off without speaking. If Mr. Kaufman was right, Libby knew she should see the best in Brittany and talk to her, but it was too late. Brittany was gone. At the same time, Libby thought as she got off at her own stop, Brittany should try and see the best in Amanda. Why couldn't she? Was it because Amanda had beat her and they'd gotten off on the wrong foot right from the start? Libby shook her head. She didn't know, but it was too good a day to worry about such things. School was over and in a week she was going to ride in a horse show and win a blue ribbon!

She couldn't wait for her early Monday morning with Ian and Amanda. She wanted to be ready, so all weekend she practiced over the cavaletti and worked on her canter to make sure Saddleshoes took the correct lead. She trotted over some small fences. She wanted Ian to notice how much she was improving.

Brittany rode both Saturday and Sunday, probably to practice for the upcoming show, Libby thought. By late Sunday afternoon, when Libby poked her head out of the tack room where she and Amanda were cleaning their saddles and bridles together, Brittany was still there in the wash stall, soaping up her brushes.

"Brittany's still here," Libby said, surprised.

Amanda rinsed out her sponge and barely registered what Libby had just said. Libby glanced at the younger girl, waiting for a reaction. Amanda pressed her lips together and furrowed her brow as she polished her stirrup irons with a cloth till they gleamed.

"It's just so strange." Libby sighed.

Amanda slid the stirrups up the leathers and pulled the straps through with a snap. She put the girth over the top of the saddle and laid a clean saddle pad over it to keep the dust off.

"That Brittany's still here, you know?" Libby waited for a comment.

"Don't pay any attention to stuff like that." Amanda

got busy on her bridle. She pressed her damp sponge into the groove in the saddle soap and rubbed it furiously. "Just think about the show."

Libby nodded and laughed a little at herself. It was silly to worry about what Brittany was doing. "You're right—the show's the only thing that matters!"

On Monday her mother was still sipping coffee and Laurel was staring sleepily at her cereal when Libby shouted good-bye. She just knew Saddleshoes would do well today. She'd been in the ring drilling the pony, doing circles and circles and circles till she was dizzy, but as soon as she and Amanda entered the ring Ian shouted to the girls, "Come on, troops, we've been going around in circles for too long. We're going out on the trails!"

Libby hesitated. The last time she had left the ring she'd gotten run away with and had fallen off. Just as things were going so well—now she was going to have to venture into the woods where Saddleshoes would think he saw scary monsters behind every tree.

"Follow me!" Ian called to the girls. "Whoever passes me has to clean my tack today!"

Amanda made a face. Ian's tack was known for not being the cleanest in the world. Libby had nothing to laugh about, though. She shortened her reins as they headed down the driveway, her heart pounding in her chest. Thick bushes lined the driveway and Saddleshoes's ears were pricked at every rustle, where he was sure goblins were about to jump out. Ian crossed the road and disappeared into the woods. Amanda went first and then Saddleshoes.

Ride confidently, Libby told herself. *You have to take the lead.* Ian had told her. She kept her legs close to the pony's sides and a firm hold on the reins. He jigged nervously in the murky forest for fear of ghosts, but she was able to stop him before he spooked. The path dropped steeply and she leaned way back as they slid onto a dirt road.

So far so good.

Amanda's loose pigtails and Cough Drop's

well-brushed-out tail bounced in time to the trot as they followed Ian. They passed a pond and Saddleshoes balked at a bridge where he thought he saw trolls, but Libby pressed her legs against his sides and the pony finally scrambled across. All three trotted single file down the dirt road under trees that grew together overhead to form a canopy, and Libby could feel the pony start to loosen up and relax. When they came out into a clearing, their eyes had to adjust to the brilliant sunlight. Before them was a sandy road that snaked around an enormous set of fields that slanted upward to a high hill. "Keep up!" Ian called to the girls as he picked up a canter. They went all the way around the fields.

Libby looked longingly at the ridge on top of the hill and wished they could ride up there, but Ian walked now and headed onto another trail. Shafts of sunlight streamed in through the foliage. Saddleshoes hopped easily over logs and trusted Libby's urgings to cross a stream even though he was sure there were gremlins.

When they got to the end of the trail Libby could see they were back where they started from.

"You see?" she said to Saddleshoes. "Nothing terrible happened to you!" Soon they were headed back up the driveway to High Hopes Horse Farm. She was almost giddy by the time they got there. "I love going out on the trails!"

"If you clean my tack I'll take you both out again on Friday," Ian said.

"No way!" Both girls laughed even though they didn't really mind at all. Now that school was over they had tons of time for things like that.

It was their first full day at the barn, and Libby and Amanda each gave their ponies soapy baths. They watched Emily jump her horse, Benson, to get ready for the show on Saturday. They cleaned all the tack on the cleaning hook, including Ian's. They hand-walked a horse of Sal's that was recovering from an injury, and they swept the entire barn floor. By four o'clock they sat outside under a tree, tired and happy.

Libby ran her hand through the grass, searching for a four-leaf clover. "I wish I could find one for good luck."

"Look!" Amanda cried. "I found one!"

Libby studied it. "Wow! I've never seen one of those."

"I guess I'm just lucky!" Amanda held it up and suddenly one of the leaves fell to the ground. Now Libby could see Amanda had just pulled two of the leaves off one piece of clover and held the stems together from another to make it look like it had four.

"Oh, it's just a fake!" Libby scoffed. She leaned against the tree and sighed. "It's going to be such a great summer, don't you think?"

Amanda made a new fake four-leaf clover and gazed at her handiwork. "The best," she muttered.

18

A SUDDEN HEADACHE

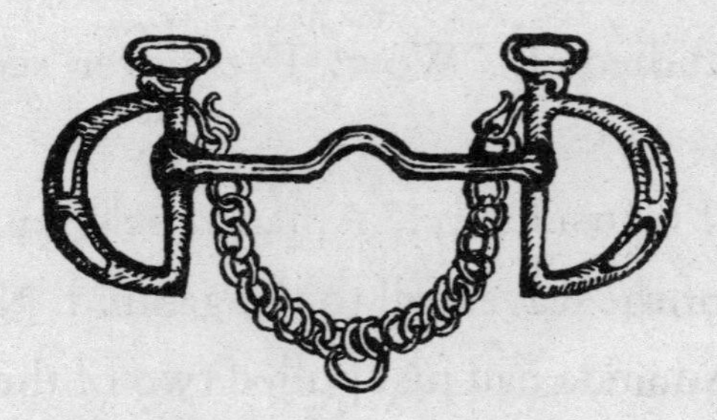

Thursday was a warm evening and the Thumps were eating dinner out on the porch. Libby reached for some dishes in a cabinet while Amanda grabbed a handful of silverware. By now she'd stayed for dinner so many times that she was practically part of the family and knew exactly where everything was. Tonight she was sleeping over so that in the morning she and Libby could go to the barn together and ride with Ian.

Mrs. Thump entered the kitchen limping. Laurel glanced up from where she was making the salad and shook her head. "You really ought to ice that knee, you know, Mom."

Mrs. Thump waved a hand.

Libby was on her way out to set the table and paused. "What's wrong?"

Her mother grabbed some napkins. "Oh, it's my knee," she said, as if it was nothing. "I'm fine—just can't run."

"You'll have to miss the race on Sunday?" Libby asked.

Mrs. Thump proceeded out to the porch. "Yes, but Laurel will still be running to represent Thumps the world over," she joked.

Libby set the plates out. She knew it was a blow for her mom not to be able to run. "You really don't care?" she asked.

"Occupational hazard, honey," she said. "There'll be other races."

Libby stared with concern at her mom's knee, which looked swollen.

"I'll probably have to go back to square one with my training, though." Her mother leaned over to look at her knee as well, and frowned. "But never mind that—are you all ready for your horse show on Saturday?"

"Yes! I can't wait!" Libby exclaimed.

"How did Saddleshoes go in your lesson on Wednesday?" Amanda carefully placed the knives and forks at each plate as she spoke.

"We jumped the brush box and the gate!" Libby said excitedly. She felt ready for her first show with the new-and-improved Saddleshoes. Just the other day Sal had watched her ride and called to her, "There's my good little jockey!" Libby was so happy to hear that from him again. "He went really well!"

Amanda pursed her lips but made no comment.

Laurel busily doled out the portions of salad onto plates. "Libby, did you jump the barrels?"

"Yep!"

"Wow! That's really good—you and Saddleshoes are really getting better." Laurel handed two plates to Amanda to put on the table. "Don't you think, Amanda?"

Amanda looked blankly at Laurel for split second as if she didn't understand, and then rearranged her expression to bring it more in line with what she was saying. "Oh, yes!"

With dinner almost ready Libby wiggled into her seat at the table. "I think Saddleshoes is going to do really well. How about Cough Drop?"

Amanda took the seat next to her. She sat erect in her chair. "He'll do fine, I'm sure."

"But you're going to have to ride him over the outside course this time." Libby knew that this was Amanda's first time jumping Cough Drop on the outside course, which was without the confines of a ring and where a lot more things could go wrong, but the younger girl seemed unfazed. "Are you nervous?"

"Not really," Amanda said, and rolled her eyes.

Libby couldn't believe how *not* nervous Amanda was and wished she could be more like her.

As soon as everyone was at the table Laurel made an announcement. "I've decided to run a half-marathon in the fall!"

"Oh no," Mrs. Thump groaned. "So that means I have to run it too. At least I'll have some time to get this knee healed."

"You'd better hurry." Laurel laughed.

"I think I've created a monster," Mrs. Thump remarked as she passed around a basket of bread, but Libby could see that her mother was proud of Laurel's newfound interest in running.

"I guess we have you two girls to thank for getting us all out of bed in the morning and starting this whole thing." Mr. Thump chuckled.

"You've both inspired us," Mrs. Thump said cheerfully. "Look at Laurel—she's running in a 5K this Sunday."

"And the horse show is on Saturday," Libby's father added, "the first day of summer."

"That's right, the longest day of the year!" Mrs. Thump dug into her salad. "We'll be there with bells on, right, Laurel?"

"Right!" Laurel agreed.

Libby grinned but her heart skipped a beat. She wanted her parents and even her sister to see her do well, and she hoped with all her heart that Saddleshoes would behave. She turned to Amanda, who was a full year younger but so oddly reserved and adultlike that Libby often found herself asking for her friend's opinion. "I'm ready, right, Amanda?"

Amanda just shrugged. "I guess so."

"I guess I'd better be ready!" Libby laughed in an effort to remain positive.

After dinner Libby scraped the plates and Amanda stacked everything in the dishwasher. Libby babbled on about the show. "So what time are your classes—mine are all in the afternoon, which I don't like because I have the whole day to worry about stuff. I just wish I rode earlier." Margaret hung around the garbage pail, her tail slowly wagging every time Libby dumped scraps off a plate into it. "I hope Saddleshoes behaves—I can't wait to jump him."

But Amanda was quiet. In fact Libby now realized that Amanda had been quiet all evening. She also looked pale. "Are you all right?" Libby asked, concerned.

Amanda sat down. "I'm getting a headache—I get these sometimes. . . ." Her voice trailed off.

Libby furrowed her brow and stood motionless in front of the other girl. "Is it going to go away?"

"When I get one of these it can last for hours." Amanda crossed her arms on the table and rested her head on them just as Mrs. Thump entered the kitchen. "Do you want to lie down, honey?" she asked.

Amanda raised her head miserably. "I think I need to go home."

Libby and her mother exchanged worried glances.

"We'll take you right away," Mrs. Thump said.

A startled look crossed Amanda's face. "Oh—no, that's all right, I'll just call my mother—"

"Don't be silly, Amanda—your mother is busy with your brother and sister. I'll take you."

"No," Amanda said firmly.

"Amanda, by the time you call your mom, we could be at your house. Now don't be silly." Mrs. Thump already had the keys in one hand and whisked Amanda out of the house and into the car before she could protest any further.

They drove to the other side of town past the hospital and a run-down convenience store. Libby wanted to ask Amanda how she felt, but when she turned around to speak Amanda was just staring out the window. Libby decided to keep quiet. Three blocks later at a boarded-up former grocery store, Amanda told Libby's mother to turn left. Old houses lined the street in various states of disrepair. A child's bike lay on its side rusting in a patch of dirt. A dog barked and strained at a rope attached to a stake in the ground. An old lady gazed at them from a chair on a sagging porch.

"Here," Amanda said. They pulled up in front of

low-slung one-story brown house surrounded by a chain-link fence with a lawn made up mostly of weeds. Two little kids watched from behind a dusty picture window and just as quickly disappeared.

Amanda muttered, "Thanks," and departed.

"I hope you feel better," Libby called to her just as the front door flew open.

Amanda's mother stood short and sturdy like a garden gnome. A dishcloth dangled from one hand. "Why didn't you phone?" she said sharply.

Amanda pushed past her without saying a word.

Mrs. Thump called from the car, "She has a headache—I thought—"

Amanda's mother yelled out a brusque "Thanks!" and vanished inside the house.

Libby turned around in her seat to look back as they drove away and realized that for as many times as Amanda had been to Libby's house, Libby had never been to hers. Did Amanda not want Libby to see her house? Libby didn't care where she lived but maybe

Amanda did. "That wasn't a very nice house," she said quietly.

"Amanda's mother has a lot on her plate with three kids and a full-time job," Libby's mother said sadly.

Libby nodded. They were such good friends but there were so many things about Amanda that Libby didn't know. Amanda had never talked about her brother or sister; in fact she never talked about anything but horses.

As soon as they got home, Laurel followed behind Libby on her way to her room. "If you ask me, I think that friend of yours, Amanda, is a lot more nervous about the show than she's letting on!"

Libby turned and said, "You're crazy, Laurel."

"Yeah, well when you were talking about how well Saddleshoes was doing, she also didn't seem that happy for you either." Laurel slipped past Libby to get to her room. "Just sayin' . . ."

"No way!" Libby shouted as she went into her own room, but to herself she considered what Laurel had said. Could Amanda be nervous? Was that why the sudden headache? Laurel was beginning to sound just like Brittany. No. Libby decided Amanda was just trying to live up to her potential—that's all—something neither Laurel nor Brittany would ever understand. Libby hoped Amanda would feel better by the morning for their ride. But in the morning when Libby got to the barn, Amanda was nowhere to be seen.

"Where's your sidekick?" Ian asked. When Libby explained Ian said, "I guess we'll have to go without her!" He walked his horse toward the gate but waited for Libby to go out first. "Come on, I'll follow you today."

Libby knew exactly where she wanted to go. She headed up the driveway and crossed onto the trail to the dirt road. She trotted past the pond and coaxed Saddleshoes over the bridge even though he didn't want to go.

"Where to?" Ian asked when they got to the fields.

Libby pointed. "Up there." She took off at a canter and called over her shoulder, "Keep up!"

They were on a narrow trail with grass that grew high on either side. Finally they reached the top and she pulled up. Below they could see High Hopes Horse Farm. Above, the sky was blue with only a white streak in the wake of a passing plane. They walked side by side along the ridge. The sun was warm and Libby could feel it on her arms. She closed her eyes and tilted her chin up to feel the heat on her face. "Oh! It's going to be such a great summer!"

"And why is that?" Ian asked.

"Because Saddleshoes is going so well now and Amanda and I will be able to ride with you all the time. It's going to be so much fun!"

"Um, I don't know, Libby," he said, and shook his head. He'd always been so funny and teasing her all the time, but suddenly he was so serious. "You shouldn't count your chickens before they hatch." He looked off into the distance and his glasses glinted in the sun.

Libby furrowed her brow. "What do you mean?"

"I took your mom's advice." He held the reins with

one hand and the other rested by his bony knee, and Libby once again thought he was probably the skinniest guy she'd ever seen. "I'm going to try again."

"For the team?" Libby squealed.

Ian nodded and his lips stretched into a grin. The horses walked quietly along and the breeze blew soft and warm. It was possibly the best moment of Libby's life to be here on the ridge with Ian and hear him say this. "That's so great!" She laughed with delight. "I know you'll make it—I just know it!"

"Do you?" Ian glanced at her and Libby thought for the first time that he looked unsure and young.

"Everybody . . . Sal . . . Emily . . . Mr. McClave . . . Amanda . . . *me* . . . We all know that you're one of the best riders *ever*!" Libby couldn't believe that Ian didn't know this about himself.

"Not everybody," Ian said bitterly.

"Well, whoever they are, they don't know anything." Then she got the best idea. "Maybe Amanda and I can groom for you—you know, when you go to all the big shows—I'll learn how to braid and we both do tack really well. Can we?"

Ian's face clouded over. "We'll see," he mumbled. "It's a long way off—you may not want to do that by then."

"Oh! I'll always want to—so will Amanda!" They headed down now and Libby added, "No matter what—you can count on us!"

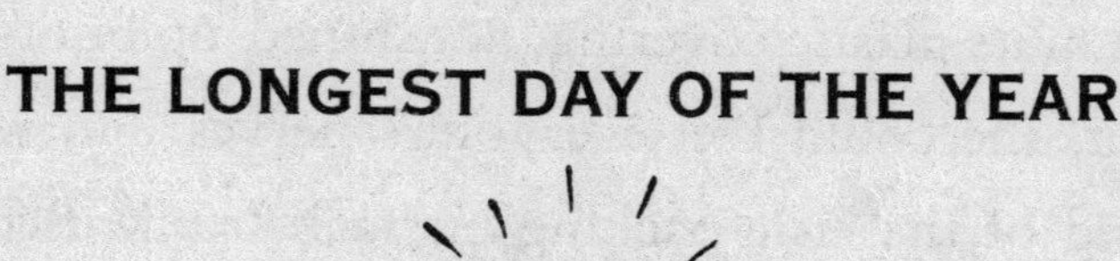

19

THE LONGEST DAY OF THE YEAR

Libby woke up the next morning to the day she'd been looking forward to all year: the first day of summer. She threw back the curtains and couldn't help being happy. It was just as beautiful outside as she'd hoped it would be.

"I'll be back with a blue ribbon later." Libby kissed Margaret on her nose. For good luck she touched the PROJECT BLUE RIBBONS sign that was still taped to her mirror before she left.

As soon she entered the barn carrying her riding jacket in its plastic covering, her shined-up boots, and helmet, she could feel everyone's nerves. Ian was at the end of the aisle packing his tack trunk. Brittany wiped a rub rag over Summer's coat. Emily led Benson out to get him on the van. He picked up each leg one at a time, higher than normal, unused to the shipping boots that had been put on him to protect his legs for the trip to the show.

"Hi, Amanda!" Libby was delighted to see her with Cough Drop on the cross ties. "You look like you're feeling all better!"

Amanda was making the finishing touches to the pony's braided mane and hardly looked up to say, "I'm fine."

Saddleshoes and Cough Drop traveled in the trailer together and Ian's two horses, plus Benson and Summer, went in Sal's van. As soon as they arrived at the show Emily got Amanda's pony off the trailer. She was in the first class and needed her number right away.

"I'll get it!" Libby sang out, and ran off to the secretary's tent. Amanda's mother arrived minutes later, her arms full of equipment. She had a bucket of brushes, hoof dressing, and rub rags and she followed her daughter around, shouting directions and wiping off her boots.

All morning Libby kept busy so she wouldn't have time to think about her stomach that was jittery with butterflies. She held Benson for Emily and put up fences in the warm-up ring. By noon she was far too excited to eat the lunch her parents had arrived with at the show. Instead she took Saddleshoes out of the trailer and hand-walked him around the show grounds to let him see everything. "Don't be afraid," she said to him when the loudspeakers went off.

She passed her parents, who waved, and Amanda's mother, who was hurrying to the outside course to watch her daughter's round.

Libby was still holding Saddleshoes when Amanda took her last trip around the outside course. She had won all her classes and had only three more fences to go. Libby watched tensely, hoping for Cough Drop to jump well as the pony headed for the split-rail fence. Good! He was over! He galloped down to the coop and she couldn't believe it was same fat pony from a few months ago. He looked fantastic and Libby knew it was all because of Amanda. As she watched him go over the last fence, she jumped up and down and cheered for them. Soon Cough Drop stood with the multicolored championship ribbon hanging from his bridle. Libby was so proud of her friend!

But Libby couldn't linger—it was time. Her equitation class was soon. She headed back to the trailer, tacked up Saddleshoes, got into her jacket, tied on her number, and headed to the ring. Her parents leaned on the rail and waved again. The judges were ready and the gate was closed. She tried to think of everything that Sal and Ian had ever told her now. It was a walk-trot-canter class and Libby knew she would have to get the pony on the right lead if she was going to win. She thought about how Ian, Emily, and Amanda looked as they rode. She sat up straight, kept her heels down, her chin up, and her hands even.

Sal watched too, along with Emily and Brittany, and even Amanda and her mother stood with Cough Drop at the other end of the ring. The class was crowded with riders but Libby knew that Saddleshoes looked better than ever and that the judges couldn't miss him even if there were a hundred other horses in the ring. "Libby doesn't pay attention." Since kindergarten, every teacher she'd ever had told her this. But Libby was determined that no one would say this to her today. She remembered her diagonals, she listened to the pony for any signals that he was going to shy, and when it was time she got him on the correct lead. When they had walked, trotted, and cantered in each direction, Libby held her breath. "Line up! All line up!" one of the judges called.

Libby stood in the line with the others. Some horses threw their heads, some backed up, some went sideways and bumped into the horse next to them. Saddleshoes's ears flicked back and forth but he stood absolutely still. They waited. Libby didn't glance at Sal, or Emily or her parents or Amanda. She sat up straight. She looked right between Saddleshoes's ears. She paid attention.

The announcer was speaking. "Today's twelve-and-under equitation . . . first place goes to Miss Libby Thump!"

She'd won! She'd actually won a blue ribbon and everyone was there to see. The judge congratulated her and slid the blue ribbon onto Saddleshoes's bridle. Libby had imagined it so many times but now it wasn't happening in her imagination. It was *really* happening! Project Blue Ribbons had been a success. Her parents whooped and Sal and Emily clapped, and she heard Brittany whistle and yell, "Way to go, Libby!" Libby craned her neck to look for Amanda and could see her and her mother leading Cough Drop back to the trailer to put him away.

Libby's jumping class was next. She had to hurry and change the pony's bit. As she walked with Sal she took off her helmet and undid her jacket to cool off. "You did so well," Sal said. "I knew you could do it—now go win that jumping class!"

"I will!" Libby assured him.

At the trailer Cough Drop had already been loaded. Amanda stood on the ramp and clipped the tail guard. In her hand she held the three blue ribbons and the large championship one.

"Congratulations!" Libby said.

"I was pleased with his last round," Amanda said without looking up.

"Aren't you excited?" Libby asked, puzzled.

Amanda busied herself with straightening up her brush box and collecting her things. "It's just a small local show, Libby. No big deal."

"Look!" Libby held up her blue ribbon proudly for Amanda to see.

Amanda hardly looked at it. "Awesome," she

replied flatly, and went on carefully placing her riding jacket in a zippered bag.

Libby didn't understand, but there was no time now. She had to get ready for her jumping class. She found the bit and was ready to change it when she suddenly realized her number was missing. "Amanda, my jumping class is next and I can't find my number—it must have fallen off when I unbuttoned my jacket!"

She had to find it. "Could you hold him while I go look?" Libby handed Saddleshoes's reins to Amanda and turned to run, when she realized she was still holding the bit. "Oh! I almost forgot!" She thrust it into Amanda's hands. "Here!"

Libby took off at a run, retracing her steps and mad at herself for being so careless. She spotted the number in the dirt right by the van where she and Sal had been talking, but as she tied it back around her waist she heard an angry voice.

She peeked around the side of the van and there were Sal and Ian. He was back in his jeans and held his two horses, who were both in their shipping boots, ready to go home. It was as if Ian had been walking away and Sal had stopped him. Ian called over his shoulder, "I'll pick up my tack trunk tomorrow," he mumbled, and Sal asked him to repeat what he'd said. Ian turned toward Sal. "I said, I'll get my tack trunk tomorrow."

Sal had his hands on his hips. "Oh no, you won't—you're not going anywhere—not without a check for this month's board!"

Ian shook his head. "I don't have it, Sal."

Libby gasped. What was Ian talking about? Was he leaving? He couldn't—he would have told her!

Sal didn't move a muscle, and when he didn't speak the younger man said, "Please, Sal. They've offered me free board at the stable over the ridge and money for as many lessons as I can teach. They've got an indoor ring and lots of jumps. It's just the great position I've been hoping for. If anybody knows how it is with horses, you do—can't you just cut me some slack? I'll pay you back. I swear I will!"

Sal took a step toward Ian and growled, "Pay your bill, Ian, then you can go wherever you want."

Ian's horse tried to back into the other one and Ian yanked on the lead, then turned back to Sal. "Please . . . Sal . . . I swear—I'll pay you when I can."

Sal pressed his lips together and looked like he was thinking. "Okay, Ian, I'll trust you. But just remember, the horse world is small."

"You mean my reputation. . . ." Ian said.

"Yep," Sal said, and walked away.

20

OFF COURSE

Libby darted behind the van and leaned against it for a second to pull herself together. How could Ian do this to Sal? He knew Sal was struggling, but she knew Ian didn't have any money either; all he wanted to do was ride. All he wanted to do was try again for the team. Libby didn't know what to think, it was so confusing.

"Libby!" Brittany's voice boomed. She came riding up on Summer. "What are you *doing*? They've already started the class! There are only two horses left before me. You're going to miss it—hurry!"

Libby felt like she was coming out of a trance. She raced back to the trailer where Amanda held Saddleshoes but all Libby could think of was what she'd just heard. "Something's happened!" Libby said breathlessly to Amanda, whose eyes grew wide. Libby took Saddleshoes from her. "I'll tell you later."

All the way to the ring Libby thought about Ian leaving so abruptly. What about their great summer? What about riding together? Going out on the trails? Grooming for him when he tried out for the equestrian team again? Had Ian known he was leaving all the time? Had he known when they'd ridden together just the other day? Why hadn't he told her? Or had he tried to tell her but she hadn't been listening? Libby looked around wildly. Her parents were on the far side of the ring waiting for her to jump; Brittany was already in the ring jumping. There was no time for Libby to warm up. She would just have to go.

Brittany cleared the last fence and people clapped, but Libby had no idea how she had done. All she knew was that they were calling her name.

"For our last ride of the day, we have Miss Libby Thump riding Saddleshoes!" Brittany passed her in the gate area and Libby heard her yell, "Libby! Wait!"

But Libby had to go. She entered the ring and it was

as if she were in a dream. She felt oddly detached from everything but as she started her circle she slowly became aware that something was wrong—terribly wrong.

She picked up a canter, came around to the first fence, and Saddleshoes gained speed. His head shot up but when she tried to hold him she had no control whatsoever. He was racing to the brush box and took off so far away from it that now he would need to put in an extra stride in order to jump the next fence. Libby tried to slow the pony down but he was out of control, and at the last minute he slid into the fence, knocking down all the rails. He had stopped! Libby couldn't

believe it. He had never stopped with her, ever. She waited as they reset the fence, so upset her mind was unable to even think straight. Then she circled around and once again the pony's head went up. He jumped the fence this time but took off after it and barreled around the corner to the third jump, which he knocked the rail off of as well. Libby stood up in her stirrups and put one hand on his mane, and with the other she pulled with all her might to make a turn to the next fence. She almost missed it, but at the last minute he jumped. She managed to turn left and jumped the gate. But someone was yelling at her. Why?

"Thank you!" the judges were calling. "You're off course!"

Libby turned the pony in a circle and finally was able to stop him.

She was supposed to jump the vertical rail fence, not the gate. She had been eliminated.

Libby dropped her reins and they walked out of the ring.

Brittany rode up to her. "Libby!" she exclaimed. "The bit! You never changed the bit! I tried to tell you!"

Libby slid off Saddleshoes and stared dumbly at the snaffle bit.

Her parents came running over. "What happened?" her mother cried.

"He didn't have the right bit in his mouth. I couldn't hold him; I forgot— " Libby said miserably.

"You forgot?" Her mother's face darkened. "You mean you weren't paying attention."

"Oh, Libby," her father said softly. Libby could see the disappointment in his eyes. Laurel looked like she felt so sorry for Libby, which Libby thought was worse than if she'd made fun of her.

Libby's mother continued, "You know, Libby, you don't pay attention and this is what happens. You could have been hurt— "

"Shh," Mr. Thump interrupted. "We'll talk it about it later."

"Sorry . . ." Libby said in a small voice. She turned to

go and over the loudspeaker she heard the announcer call out the winners for her class.

"In first place, riding Summer, is . . ." Brittany had won.

Libby watched as the judge pinned the blue ribbon on Summer's bridle. Brittany leaned over and shook the judges' hands. Sal and Emily stood at the gate with a group of people who congratulated them. Project Blue Ribbons had turned out the way Libby had wanted. All three of Sal's students had won first place ribbons, and Libby knew it would help High Hopes Horse Farm.

But it still hadn't turned out well for Libby, and she thought back to when she left Amanda with Saddleshoes. Hadn't she handed her the bit? Why didn't Amanda put it on? She knew Saddleshoes always jumped in it.

In the distance Libby watched Ian load one of his horses onto another stable's van. He had spent an entire month at Sal's barn without paying. She thought of the show where she'd first told him about High

Hopes, and now she wished she'd never even met him.

Suddenly Libby spotted Amanda and her mother leaving as well.

"Amanda! Amanda!" Libby shouted, and ran after her. She had to tell her what had happened. The girl turned and looked at Libby with no expression. It was the look of a stranger who you've just mistaken for a friend.

"We're in a hurry, Amanda!" her mother barked, and then walked briskly to the car.

"I can't talk now," Amanda said.

Libby didn't understand. "Okay, well, see you at the barn—"

Amanda shook her head robotically. "I'm not going to the barn. From now on I'm riding with Ian at another stable."

From now on? No, Libby thought. How could Amanda not be going to High Hopes anymore? They were supposed to be riding together all summer. They were supposed to be great riders someday. It was going to be a battle and they were buddies—

war buddies—just like Mr. McClave had said.

Libby had to repeat what Amanda said in order to try to understand what she was hearing. "You're riding with Ian? At another stable?"

"Yes." Amanda pulled in her chin authoritatively.

"What do you mean?" Libby whispered, utterly bewildered.

"You're lucky—you already have so much," Amanda said unemotionally. "Riding doesn't matter to you the way it does to me."

"But I thought we were friends," Libby blurted out.

Amanda had her arms folded tightly. "My mom says that all I need to do is think about my riding. If I do, my mom says I'll be a really good rider and maybe even get to ride in the Olympics someday. That's all I care about."

"But we can ride together like we have been," Libby said softly.

"Face it, Libby," Amanda replied. "You're never going to be a really good rider."

Libby stood holding Saddleshoes, speechless. Of all the things that Amanda had said, that it didn't matter to her, that Libby was lucky—lucky to have a nice home, something that Amanda didn't have—was hard to hear, but it was like a knife to her heart to hear her friend say that Libby would never be a really good rider.

Parents and trainers and kids with ponies all milled around Libby. As Amanda walked away the girl's ribbons fluttered in her back pocket. Libby called to her, "How do you know?"

"I just do!" Amanda said without turning around.

21
STARTING OVER

That night the Thump family went out for dinner, but Libby wasn't hungry and instead went to her room.

"Just leave her alone," she could hear her mother say as they left. The door shut, voices faded, the car drove away, and the house became quiet.

Libby sat on her bed and stewed. Margaret lay next to her with her head between her paws, staring sadly off into space. In Libby's hand was the satin ribbon that she had so badly wanted to win. It was a beautiful shade of royal blue. "First Place" was stamped in gold into the center of the rosette.

She had come so close. She had won her first class. Then with everyone rooting for her and watching, she had blown it. She crossed the room and let the ribbon drop into the trash. Then she took the sign off the mirror and put that in there too. Libby went back to her bed.

"I'm never going to a really good rider," she said out loud, and tears rolled down her cheeks, because even though Amanda had not changed the pony's bit Libby knew it was still her own fault. She hadn't been paying attention . . . again.

Libby's eyes traveled to all the drawings on the wall and she wondered, was she a better artist than rider? Should she give up riding now and put all her energy into her drawing?

Libby then thought: What do you do when you try to live up to your potential and you find out that you have no potential in the one thing you love to do? Or when you find out that someone who you thought was your friend really wasn't your friend after all?

Or when you've wanted nothing more than to win a blue ribbon but when you finally win one you realize that the only place it belongs is in the trash?

Libby stewed and Margaret stewed along with her.

Later, when everyone was back from dinner, Laurel stood in the doorway. "What's this?" She took the blue ribbon out of the trash. When Libby didn't answer, Laurel hung it back on top of the mirror.

Libby waited until the sound of her sister's flip-flops disappeared down the hallway, and then she got up and took the ribbon off the mirror and put it back in the trash.

The next day Laurel won her race.

"Congratulations," Libby muttered.

She lugged beach chairs and umbrellas through the beach club for her mom, whose knee was still bothering her. When all the lugging and the annual cleaning of the locker was done, Libby stole away to look at the ocean. She stood at the metal railing and watched the waves.

"Hey, Libby!" a voice called. It was her old best friend Mim. She was loaded down with beach bags. "You did it!" Mim's cheeks were pink and she was a little out of breath. "Brit told me—you won yesterday! You must be so happy!"

Libby shook her head. It was hard to say out loud what a complete mess she had made of her jumping class. Libby knew she didn't deserve good-natured Mim's sympathy, either, but she also realized just how good it was to have somebody to talk to and how much she had missed her friend. "My jumping class was a complete disaster. Saddleshoes stopped, he was knocking down rails all over the place, I couldn't hold him, we went off course, and got eliminated."

Mim dumped her bags by her feet. She pushed out her bottom lip and looked puzzled. "But Brit said that you were jumping Saddleshoes so well."

"We *were* jumping well. . . ." Libby was about to explain when out of nowhere Brittany came roaring up to the girls. "LIBBY!" She squeezed in between Mim and Libby. Libby tried to congratulate Brittany for her win at the show but Brittany talked right over her. "You will never guess—Amanda left the barn!"

Brittany was overjoyed at Amanda's sudden departure from High Hopes, but a moment later her expression changed and her voice grew serious. "Libby, there's something else." Brittany bit her lip and looked like she had bad news. "Sal said that Kate's coming back . . . tomorrow."

Libby's heart fell. She'd been so wrapped up in the show and Ian and Amanda leaving that she'd forgotten about the possibility of Kate coming back.

"Is Kate taking Saddleshoes away with her?" Mim asked, concerned.

Libby nodded. Now the full impact of losing her pony forever came hurtling toward her. "I'll see you guys later." Libby quickly walked away.

"Libby!" Mim called.

"I'm sorry!" Brit yelled.

Libby stared out the window on the way home from the beach.

The summer was ruined.

"Everything all right, honey?" her mother asked.

No. Everything wasn't all right. "I'm fine," Libby said, even though she wasn't. As soon as she got home she ran to her room and went to the trash for the blue ribbon. It was the one thing that she would always have to remember Saddleshoes with. She was sorry now that she'd thrown it out and had to find it, but when she looked, her trash can was empty. Her mother must have emptied the trash. She raced to the garage determined to plunge all the way up to her elbows in garbage in order to find that ribbon. She yanked off the lid of the can only to see it, too, was empty. And that's when she remembered that the garbage was always picked up on Monday mornings.

The ribbon was gone. Probably at the dump lying

under hundreds of pounds of garbage by now.

She shuffled inside and flopped into a kitchen chair, completely miserable.

Her mother hobbled in and went to the freezer to get her ice pack. She sat down and rested her leg out in front of her on another chair to ice her knee.

"Well isn't this a fine kettle of fish?" she said to no one in particular.

Libby propped her chin up on one hand. "Amanda left the barn," she said quietly. "Ian's not coming back either . . . and Kate's taking Saddleshoes, so basically I have nothing to ride for the entire summer."

Her mother's hand went to her mouth. "Oh, Libby."

Libby could feel the tears coming. "What am I going to do?" she cried.

Her mother rearranged the ice on her knee and then looked Libby in the eye. "Start over," she said firmly.

"Start over?" Libby moaned.

"That's right. You are going to have to begin all over again—that's how life sometimes is, Libby." She pointed to her knee. "Everybody at some point or other has to do it. I'm doing it right now; your father has had to do it by working for someone else." Her mother reached over to smooth her hair. "It's not the worst thing, honey."

"But how?" Libby sniffed.

"You're going to ask Sal if he has another horse for you to ride, and if he doesn't, then you are going to have to watch and learn that way. And if you don't want to do that then I guess it was never really that important to you in the first place."

"But what about Amanda and Ian? I thought we were friends, but I was wrong." Libby could feel a whole new round of tears about to come pouring out of her eyes with this horribly disappointing thought.

"Oh, honey don't cry," Libby's mother said. "You do have friends—good friends—in Brittany and Mim."

Libby looked down. She hadn't been a very good friend to either one of them lately.

Libby dried her tears with her sleeve.

Mrs. Thump rearranged the ice on her knee. "You and Brittany and Mim have known one another since you were practically born. You've shared so much together—you will always have that special bond."

"Like war buddies," Libby said quietly.

"War buddies?" Mrs. Thump laughed.

Libby sat up a little taller in her chair to explain. "Mr. McClave says that he and General George have been through so much that they're old war buddies—like in combat, when all you have are your buddies who have your back and they're relying on you, too. Mr. McClave says that these are the friendships that you never forget."

"And that you never take for granted," Mrs. Thump added.

"I won't. Not ever again." Libby pushed herself up from the table. "I hope your knee feels better, Mom."

Mrs. Thump waved a hand. "It will!" she sang out.

Just as Libby left the room her mother called over her shoulder, "And Libby, you might want to look in

my nightstand in the bottom drawer. There's something in there for you."

Libby ran to the bedroom and slid open the drawer, and there was her blue ribbon wrapped up in tissue, safe and sound.

22

OVER THE RIDGE

Libby woke early. The rest of the house was silent. Everyone was still sleeping but she knew that it would be Saddleshoes's last day at High Hopes Horse Farm and she didn't want to miss a second of it. She dressed, tiptoed out of the house before light, and made her way quickly through the early morning mist to the barn.

Princess galloped up to meet her.

"Hello, beautiful," Libby said softly, and fed her a carrot.

Libby ran a hand over the mare's shoulder, back, and rump and knew that she'd been so determined to win a blue ribbon that she hadn't paid any attention to the big white horse recently . . . but someone had. "Who's been taking care of you?" Libby wondered out loud. The horse's shaggy winter coat was gone and her sleek, shiny summer one had come in beautifully. Her mane had been pulled and there were no burrs in her tail.

With Princess following, Libby walked down the hill to the mare's shed. There on the shelf was her old grooming kit covered in cobwebs and dust. Libby guiltily took it with her to clean all the brushes and let herself out the gate. As she passed the empty ring she tried not to think about Ian and how he always called her his "jump-crew fairy." When she entered the barn the aisle looked strangely forlorn without Amanda there fussing over Cough Drop on the cross ties. She would never again hear her talk excitedly about growing up and being on the equestrian team. They would never, ever again go out on the trails together.

Practically overnight everything had changed.

Libby ducked into the tack room and hoped that having three students from the stable win had helped Sal, but with Saddleshoes and Ian's two horses leaving, there would be three more empty stalls. It made her angry all over again at Ian for walking out and not paying. How could he have done this to Sal? Libby wished she could tell Ian what she really thought—that he was a quitter . . . that he probably had quit going to the equestrian team training session just like he had quit Sal's.

She gathered all her tack and was about to leave when something shiny caught her eye. It was hanging off the cleaning hook. It was the bit—the kimberwick that Ian had given her. She snatched it along with her riding helmet and could feel her heart start to hammer against her ribs, because there was no way she could stop herself from what she was about to do.

Saddleshoes called to her from the end of the aisle and she hurried to him.

She quickly got the pony ready to go and left the barn as if she was just going to ride in the ring like she had all the other mornings. Libby looked around to see if Emily or Sal were anywhere near. They were both busy cleaning stalls. She was never supposed to go out on her own—no one was—but Libby was going to find Ian. She was going to find him now!

With the coast clear she headed down the driveway. She rode the pony across the road and into the woods along the same path she had ridden just a few days ago with Ian. To think she had been so happy that day to hear all about how he was going to try for the team again, when the entire time he knew he was leaving. Libby cringed at how she'd suggested that she and Amanda should groom for him. She came to the bridge and Saddleshoes went right across, then she urged him onto the dirt road with the bit that had grown warm in her hand.

She cantered up the hill to the top of the ridge and stopped to look down. A breeze picked up and tousled the pony's mane. *Over the ridge*, she thought—that was where Ian had told Sal he was going. If she was right the stable was at the end of a trail on the other side of this hill. She squinted her eyes to see if there was a trail below. Where was it?

There! In the corner of the field was an opening in the trees. Libby scanned the horizon and could see the top of what could be an indoor ring at the edge of the clearing in the woods. She kicked Saddleshoes and they went down the hill, and a moment later they were on the trail. When she came to the end of the path she was in an open field. Across from her in a driveway by a large, brand-new horse barn was the battered old red Ford pickup.

"Ian!" she shouted. He was in the ring lunging his horse as he had the very first morning she saw him at Sal's.

His horse spooked at her voice and Ian quickly gathered in the lunge to calm it.

Libby pulled up to the rail of the ring and looked around. It was the opposite of High Hopes. Everything was top of the line. The ring was level with perfect footing. The jumps were numerous and freshly painted. The manicured paddocks each had one sleek show horse quietly grazing. Bright flowers spilled out of large planters that decorated each side of the barn door.

"Here!" Libby said, and tossed the bit at Ian's feet.

Ian bent down wearily to pick it up. "I gave it you, Libby, it's yours to keep," he said sadly.

Libby could hardly breathe. "Why didn't you show up for the equestrian team training session, Ian? Did you *quit* that too—just like you *quit* Sal's?"

Ian walked to the fence and leaned his arms against it. His horse stood behind him and didn't stir. All was quiet. "Yes." Ian cast his eyes down at his arms, which were folded on the top rail of the fence. He didn't speak for a full minute, and Libby was about to turn and go home, when he began to speak. "It happened right before I had been chosen for the training session. I was a working student for a former equestrian team rider who ran one of the top show barns in the country.

There were other working students there my age as well, and it was very competitive. It was also an incredible chance to ride with someone as good as this guy. But the longer I was there, the more I didn't like him. I thought he had a mean streak and I didn't agree with some of his methods. We butted heads. One day we all went out on the young horses. I was riding a small chestnut—a three-year-old who barely knew how to jump. We came to a fallen-down tree on the side of the field and he told me to take the horse over it. I didn't feel my horse was ready, but he insisted. Sure enough it stopped. He became very angry and said I was ruining his young horse. He practically dragged me off the horse and got on him himself. After many tries he got him over the jump. The poor horse was terrified, and blowing, and soaked with sweat. He got off and threw the reins at me in front of the other students and said, 'You'll never make it past the first day at the team.' It was humiliating and the last straw, so I left. Never showed up for the training session and didn't ride for an entire year."

Libby sat speechless on her pony.

"I'm sorry, Libby." Ian raised his head and looked her in the eyes. "I know you think I'm a good rider . . . but I'm not perfect—I've made mistakes." He straightened up.

Ian was right, he had made mistakes, but Libby knew there was no denying she had as well. She'd lost her number at the show, had forgotten to put the right bit on Saddleshoes. She had thought that Saddleshoes was an awful pony when he was really just afraid. And Amanda? Libby wasn't sure.

"Amanda says I'll never be a really good rider," Libby blurted out. "Is she right?"

"Don't listen to Amanda," Ian said. "Her mother puts too much pressure on her to win."

"But Amanda is loaded with talent!" Libby exclaimed.

"She doesn't believe it; that's the only reason she said that to you." He pushed himself away from the fence. "Just work hard, Libby, and don't give up when things get tough and don't listen to people when they say you can't do something—like I did." Ian shook the sand off the bit. He leaned over the fence and handed it to her.

Libby reached out and took the bit. "Thanks for all the help you gave me with Saddleshoes—I really learned a lot."

Ian gave her the crooked smile. "I think I learned more."

She watched as he made his way to the center of the ring to give a lesson.

Amanda entered through the gate riding a pretty bay pony with her mother right behind. Her handbag fell off her shoulder and she fumbled with the strap to get it back on. "Amanda!" she yelled. "Sit up straight! You look like a sack of potatoes!"

Libby suddenly felt sorry for the younger girl.

Amanda glanced timidly in Libby's direction. Libby took a hand off the rein for a second and uncurled her fingers in a tentative greeting. Amanda paused and then did the same. Her mother hollered, "Amanda! Did you hear me? What's wrong with you today?"

Libby turned Saddleshoes for the trip back to High Hopes. Amanda had been right about one thing after all; it *did* matter more to her than it ever would to Libby to win blue ribbons.

23

JUMP!

Libby rode the brown-and-white pony back the way they'd come. She grasped the bit firmly in her hand. Even though she wouldn't be needing it anymore because the pony was going back to his owner, she promised herself that she would keep it forever to remember this time of riding Saddleshoes and Ian's story.

She led the pony into the barn, afraid that Sal or Emily would be there waiting to scold her for leaving the property alone, but they were both rushing around too busy to notice that she'd even been gone. In fact everybody was already at the barn this morning. Mr. McClave was getting General George out of his stall to groom him. Brittany poked her head out of Summer's stall.

Libby stopped to apologize. "Listen, Brittany . . ." She was unsure of where to begin.

"It's all right." Brittany stood by Summer's head, holding a brush.

"No. It's not." Libby continued, "I'm sorry for the way I've been acting."

Brittany ran the brush against the palm of her hand. "I probably shouldn't have told you those things about Amanda. . . ."

Libby knew now that Brittany had been telling the truth. "You were right. Amanda's mother did try to get Saddleshoes for Amanda to ride. I think Amanda wanted to win so bad, she had gone along with it."

"I think so too," Brittany said, but then she shifted her weight to the other foot and looked away. "There's just one thing, Libby . . . and I hope you won't be mad at me . . ."

Libby's mind reeled. What was Brittany trying to say? Was it something else about Amanda? Or the show?

"It's about Princess," Brittany finally said. "You've been so busy trying to ride Saddleshoes and everything . . . and . . . um . . . Princess needed grooming and everything and um . . ."

"That was *you*?" Libby said incredulously.

Brittany scrunched up her nose. "That was me—you're not mad, are you?"

"No!" Libby exclaimed. A year ago she would have been angry, but not now. She never thought that Brittany even cared that much about horses—not like Libby, anyway. She thought that riding to Brit was just another sport and horses were just another sport accessory, like a hockey stick or a soccer ball. Libby knew for sure she'd been wrong about Brittany. They *had* shared a lot together, and if it was possible for two girls like them to be "war buddies," than she and Brittany were that. "So . . . best friends again, Brit?"

Brittany looked up at the rafters in relief. "Best friends, Lib."

Sal came rushing down the aisle toward them with a wheelbarrow full of shavings and called as he passed, "Kate's coming—she'll be here any minute. Don't put Saddleshoes away yet, Libby—I want her to see you jump him!"

Libby led the pony to his stall to change his bit. *So it would come in handy one more time after all,* she thought sadly. She took a deep breath and exhaled slowly. After this morning she would have to start over. Even if there was no horse for her to ride at Sal's she would come to the barn every day and do stalls and clean tack and watch.

As she fiddled with the buckles on the bridle, Libby thought of her father taking a new job and her mother with her knee, unable to run. She thought of Sal and hoped that she'd been able to help out just a

little with her measly blue ribbon. Libby thought of her sister Laurel's running and finding out that she'd had potential all along and didn't even know it . . . till now. She thought of Ian trying again for the team. Last she thought of Amanda, with all her potential but with hurdles to get over that Libby would never have to face.

Libby put the bridle back on Saddleshoes. She looked into the pony's eyes and held the bit with both hands. "Kate's coming to take you back with her . . . but don't forget me, all right? Because I will never forget you." The pony nudged her and rested his chin on Libby's shoulder, and she rubbed his nose.

There was the sound of crunching gravel on the driveway, and when she looked out Saddleshoe's stall window, sure enough a truck and trailer bounced over the rutted ground. She kissed him one last time. "Sal was right," she whispered. "You *were* a good teacher." Then she led him down the aisle and out of the barn for the last time.

The trailer came to a halt and a girl jumped out of the driver's seat.

"Libby!" Kate called to her. "I see you've taken good care of my pony for me!"

Libby nodded but her throat was so tight, she couldn't speak.

Sal came out of the barn. He took down the ramp.

Libby gasped.

Inside the trailer were two horses! Libby watched, stunned, as Sal helped Kate back them off.

"What do you think, Libby?" Kate said, proudly holding one while Sal held the other.

"They're beautiful—but—" Libby stammered.

"There's no better trainer anywhere than Sal, so my aunt sent me back with these guys—if I do a good job she says she'll send more!"

Libby knew what this could mean for Sal and Emily and High Hopes. With really good horses coming to the stable, it could be a whole new beginning.

"What about Saddleshoes?" Libby was almost afraid to ask, because she knew her parents could never afford to buy the pony, but she had to know:

"Are you going to sell him?"

"I've actually found someone to ride him now," Kate said, and exchanged glances with Sal.

"You have?" Libby said anxiously.

Sal nodded. "Yep. She's almost twelve years old and a really good rider." Sal put his hand on Libby's shoulder. "And that's you, Libby."

"For real?" Libby could hardly believe her ears.

"For real," Kate said. "You can ride him for as long as you want, just as if he were your own pony."

Mr. McClave, Emily, and Brittany gathered outside to admire the new horses.

"I'll bet this one can jump the moon." Mr. McClave chuckled.

Brittany turned to Libby. "I'll go get Summer and we can ride together." Soon Libby and Brittany were both riding around the ring.

"Shorten your reins, girls!" Sal called to them as he set up fences while Kate watched.

Saddleshoes shied and Libby ran a hand down his

neck to calm him. She sat up a little taller, pushed her shoulders back, and smiled. She had accomplished her goal and won a blue ribbon, but Libby couldn't help thinking that she'd probably learned a whole lot more from the blue ribbon that she hadn't won.

Maybe it wasn't going to be such a bad summer after all. Her skin tingled as she headed for the first fence and Saddleshoes lengthened his stride, one . . . two . . . three . . . jump! The pony took off over the fence, they were up in the air, and it was like flying.

Some riding terms that you may want to know

bay horse: "bay" is a way to describe the hair coat color of a reddish brown horse with a black mane and tail and lower legs.

bolt: when a horse bolts it takes off suddenly at a gallop and is very difficult to stop. This can happen if it is startled by something. It is also an evasion of what the rider is asking it to do.

canter: natural three-beat gait that all horses have.

cavaletti: rails placed in a row on the ground about three to three-and-a-half feet apart. Cavaletti are used as a schooling exercise for horses to improve their balance and strength. They're also used as a good introduction for the beginner rider to learn how to jump.

cross ties: device made of rope or chain or rubber lines that are attached to the wall in a barn at one end and the other end is clipped to the horse's halter on both sides. You would cross tie a horse as a way to keep it still while it's being groomed.

curried: when you've "curried" a horse you've used the currycomb to groom it. The currycomb is used in a circular motion to lift the dirt and dander away from the skin. After using the currycomb you would use the dandy brush to brush away the loosened dirt.

diagonals: the horse trots in a two-beat gait with the legs moving in diagonal pairs so that, for example, if the right foreleg and the left hind leg moved forward, the left foreleg and the right hind leg would be moving backward. To be on the correct diagonal while you're posting (rising and sitting in the saddle) depends on which direction the horse is going on the circle. If you're going to the left you would rise out of the saddle when the horse's outside, or right leg, was moving forward. You would sit when the right leg was moving backward.

equitation: the art of how the rider looks and how effective the rider is at riding a horse. A lot of emphasis is placed on the position of the rider, and in a horse show it's the rider that is being judged in an "equitation" class more so than the horse.

in-and-out: term to describe two jumps spaced one or two strides apart. An in-and-out is very often used as part of a cavaletti.

kimberwick: a type of metal bit with "D" rings and a curb chain that is secured behind the horse's chin. The kimberwick bit is used with one rein.

lunge line: a device used for ground training the horse where the rider holds the lunge line that is attached to the horse's bridle as the horse travels around him in a circle. The lunge line can be used for many different purposes but it's a great way to teach a horse voice commands.

riding crop: sometimes called a "bat," is a type of whip that is used to back up natural aids such as the voice or the legs. A crop can be used as a reprimand, but only by a more advanced rider.

shied: a horse is said to have "shied" when it has been startled by something and moves suddenly. Horses will jump away from, or "shy" at whatever frightens them.